The Circus

The Circus

Skeletons in the Cupboard Series Book 4

A.J. Griffiths-Jones

FOR SYLVIA

Author's Note

It goes without saying that my characters are all fictional, although I admit to adding certain traits and secrets from the people I meet. Life is far too colourful not to integrate fact with fiction.

This book is dedicated to a wonderful lady, who has always been a part of my life, my aunt Sylvia Caswell. Not only does she have a larger than life personality, but she is hugely talented too. Each design on my book cover started out as an oil painting in Sylvia's studio, slowly bringing to life the towns and villages that I described to her and adding her own beautiful landscapes. Not only do I owe gratitude to my Aunt Sylvia for creating such vibrant scenes, but she has always been the voice of reason when I needed advice, although we invariably end up giggling so much that our eyes are filled with tears and our hearts full of happiness. We share a love of Bohemian fashion and often compare our finds from little boutiques, sometimes even swapping clothes and of course my love of books has definitely been inherited from Aunt Sylvia who devours literature with a passion. She is a rock with a heart of gold.

Of course, my cousin Antony Caswell plays a major part in the design process too, with his technical expertise, as do the team at Creativia, who work tirelessly to produce, deliver and promote my books. It is the sheer enthusiasm of the people around me that keeps me writing, so to friends, acquaintances and relatives across the world, I thank you all.

It was an easy decision to set this book, the fourth in my cosy mystery series, in a travelling show. I knew that the characters would be bold and independent, each with their own particular talent but also capable of withholding their individual secrets. It's a weird process, creating the lives of strangers and then committing them to paper but, once the story begins, I simply write what I see in my imagination and follow the tale to the end. In all honesty I never know where the characters will take me, but they always surprise me and never fail to disappoint.

Finally, a big thank you to Jason 'Danger' McNeill who was not only the inspiration behind a certain character in this work but also kindly agreed to read through the finished manuscript to give much needed feedback.

Contents

Prologue

The year is 1985. In America, Ronald Reagan is beginning his second term as President of the United States, something which leaves the British public in awe, wondering how a B-list actor can find himself in one of the most important roles of his life, a sign that things are changing across the globe.

In the United Kingdom, teenagers are exploring new fashions, from padded shoulders inspired by the actresses on the drama 'Dallas' to tennis gear as worn on the courts of Wimbledon in the summer. In January of this particular year, British Telecom announced its plans to phase out the iconic red telephone boxes across the country, causing an outcry by the public, who saw them as a part of our heritage. The Royal family were in the news too, with visits to far off lands and rumours of marital troubles for Prince Charles and Princess Diana, a woman who had captured the hearts of every household with her demure looks and tireless campaigning for charities overseas.

The mid 1980's also prompted a change in one of the nation's much loved entertainments, the Circus. People were becoming more aware of the cruelty involved in trying to tame the lions and tigers who were forced to perform nightly in the ring, and the circus owners themselves were forced to look for new acts, with human performers, to replace the traditional animal ones. Enter the daredevil stunt riders, flying through rings of fire on their motorcycles, strong men able to lift three times their own bodyweight and everyone's favourite, the fortune-teller, peering into her crystal ball and conjuring up promises that she sensed her customers wanted to hear, as long as they crossed her palm with a princely sum of money.

It is this strange travelling troupe that I want to introduce you to now. Performers relying upon each other for companionship and support, knowing that night after night they would have to give their work every ounce of energy, smiling for the crowds that flocked to see, and retiring to their caravans and trailers long past midnight, exhausted, hungry and with ears still tingling from the cheers of their captive audience. And then of course, there were the secrets, things that were hidden from public view but secrets all the same!

Chapter One

Psychic Sheila

Lounging back against the vibrantly coloured silk cushions inside her caravan, Sheila Hannigan sucked deeply on a filtered cigarette. It was her fifth one that morning but she didn't care as there was nobody around to reprimand her and no glaring eyes to shoot disapproving looks. She toyed with the idea of getting up to make a cup of tea, but couldn't be bothered, and instead reached for the red wine that lay within her grasp on a narrow shelf. There were no glasses close to hand, so Sheila swigged the liquid down straight from the neck of the bottle, closing her eyes as she did so and letting the alcohol hit the back of her throat.

"Feck!" the woman shouted, as the caravan jolted, causing her to spill wine down her chin and on to her frilly white blouse, "Fecking Hell!"

Replacing the bottle on the shelf, Sheila pulled back the curtains and peered outside. She'd almost forgotten that the caravan was mobile, being towed along by a flat-bedded truck piled high with poles and tents, and now she could see that they'd left the main road and were heading down a bumpy country lane. Stubbing out her cigarette in a bone china ashtray, Sheila realised that they must be getting close to the next site, where over the next twenty-four hours everyone would work tirelessly to set up the big top and get ready for yet another opening night at the circus. This was her life and she wouldn't change it for anything, although there were certain things that she might like to add to it.

After another ten minutes of bumping along, the convoy pulled on to a vast field bordered by traditional stone walls. They were close to the edge of a town, as they always tried to be, and throngs of children had lined the streets as the caravans, trailers, trucks and lorries rolled past, each little face lighting up at the prospect of being taken to see the amazing performers. Many of the spectators had waved and, as was their duty to the public, the travelling group had smiled and raised their hands in acknowledgment, all except for Sheila that was. It was illegal to travel inside a caravan whilst it was in motion therefore, in order to avoid police detection, she had kept herself hidden away behind the violet coloured curtains. The only hint of the occupant's talents was the paintwork on the outside of her little home, displaying the words 'Psychic Sheila' in bold Italics, a talent for which she was both popular and renowned. It helped that she had the inherent gipsy fortune-teller looks too, with long curly black hair and dark eyes that had the ability to look deep into a person's soul. Sheila had proved her worth over and over and now, every time they revisited a town, the same faces would appear at her door seeking news of their fate. Lucky for her they were willing to pay generously to hear what 'Psychic Sheila' had to say but, by the time she had given the circus owner his cut and bought her weekly indulgences, there was never enough left to make a significant impact on her retirement fund and so Sheila stayed on year after year.

Rap, rap, rap at the door.

"Wait a minute," Sheila yelled, pulling off her blouse and grabbing a clean one, "I'm getting changed."

"Come on woman," a deep male voice with a Dublin accent shouted from outside, "We're going to get something to eat before we set up. Are you coming or not?"

Sheila unlocked the door and peered out. She immediately came face to face with the rugged good looks of Roland, otherwise known as 'The Great Rolando Circus Master'. He and his father, Roland Senior, were the only other Irish people in the troupe and Sheila felt a close kinship, although she disapproved of his reputation with the ladies.

"Well?" she said, putting one hand on her hip, "What's the hurry?"

"There's a café just down the road," Roland smiled, "Reckon we should get there before the lunchtime crowd, otherwise they might not be able to fit us all in."

Sheila snorted and reached for her purse, "You go on, but would you bring me a hot bacon sandwich?"

The man smiled, showing perfect white teeth, "Don't be daft woman, I don't want your money. You can pay me in kind later on."

Sheila blushed. Roland always had this effect on her. "Go on with you," she laughed, "See you later."

Retreating inside, the gipsy woman stood with her back against the caravan door listening to the hunk of a man calling to someone across the field. It was fantastic how everyone got along, she thought, just like a proper family. It didn't seem to matter where people came from, and they were a pretty international group, everyone was made to feel just as welcome as the next. Sometimes, but not very often, Sheila wondered what ordinary folk thought about the travelling circus. She would put a large bet on people thinking it was the best job in the world. Hadn't her father once made a joke about everyone wanting to run away to join the circus? Sheila was certain he had, but it was so long ago that she couldn't be absolutely sure.

Turning to look in the mirror, Sheila saw a pale face looking back at her. It was a pretty face, but without make-up she looked older than her forty-five years. She sighed and opened a drawer, revealing blusher pots, eyeshadow palettes, mascara, foundation and every shade of lipstick under the sun. This was her favourite time of day, where she could sit alone and transform herself from just plain old Sheila Hannigan into 'Psychic Fortune-Teller Extraordinaire'. It usually took an hour, as besides the application to her face, there was a suitable outfit to choose, a bandana with gold coins attached to tie over her thick locks and her signature black lace gloves to put on. The end result was very pleasing, both to Sheila and to her fans.

By one o'clock Roland and his buddies had returned and, on seeing Sheila's caravan door flung wide open, he stepped inside her home without knocking.

"One fresh bacon roll," he grinned.

"Bloody hell," she cursed, quickly pulling down her flouncy skirt, "Don't you ever knock?"

"Sorry Sheila, how was I to know you were adjusting your stockings! The door was wide open."

"Well, you ought to know better Roland O'Hare. Never enter a ladies chamber uninvited."

"Ah Sheila, come on," he soothed, "Any chance of a cuppa?"

"Not until you've earned it," she scolded, "There are tents to put up and allsorts yet."

Roland nodded and winked as he set the bacon roll down on the worktop, "Rain check darling."

Outside on the field work was well underway. The trucks were being unloaded and men rushed here and there, hammering, pulling, constructing and shouting. The crew had setting up down to a fine art these days, but it was after many years of experience and the effort was still exhausting. They had a day and a half to get things ready for opening night and the checklists were endless. Besides the big top, there were smaller tents to construct for the sideshows, safety wires to install for the acrobats, candy floss and toffee apple carts to get going and seating to set up for the hundreds of visitors who would flock to the show over the coming week.

Sheila had a second responsibility to her fellow performers, albeit unofficial and self-appointed, she was chief seamstress, fixing ripped seams, making adjustments and generally making good on the wear and tear of the spectacular costumes worn to mesmerize the audience. Her trusty black Singer sewing machine could often be heard spinning its wheel as she turned it at full speed, while very often a half-clothed performer waited patiently for their last minute alteration to be completed. Although by no means the oldest member of the travelling circus, Sheila felt that her status as tailor gave her a motherly quality that the others looked up to. It also meant that during their time together in her caravan, the fortune-teller would often get to find out about the worries, indiscretions and troubles of her fellow circus family. As was her nature, Sheila always listened politely, giving sound advice when it was asked for and never reprimanding. Although, on occasion, she had been very tempted to intervene, especially when the goings-on affected other members of the group, but all in all Sheila was very good at keeping secrets.

The fortune-teller looked over at the pile of costumes waiting to be repaired and altered, enough to keep her busy for the next few hours, but first she needed to devour the warm bacon roll, make a pot of tea and smoke one more cigarette. It was the small pleasures in life that made Sheila content with her lot and God help anyone who threatened to stand in the way of her peace.

The Irishwoman switched on her portable television set while she waited for the kettle to boil, silently thanking Roland O'Hare for hooking her caravan up to the electricity supply the moment they'd arrived. Catching the end of the lunchtime news, Sheila listened intently.

"THERE IS NOW ONE EXTRA SECOND ADDED TO THE CALENDAR YEAR," the presenter proudly announced.

"Well feck," Sheila cursed, "What the Devil use is that?"

She stood munching the roll, listening intently as the story unfolded. Within minutes it was over.

"Sheila?" a shrill voice cried, accompanied by a light tapping on the door, "Are you in?"

"Of course I'm in," she answered, inviting the visitor inside, "Where else would I be?"

A slim, beautiful woman stepped into the caravan. She was clutching a metallic gold leotard.

"Are you being busy?" the young woman asked, her English grammar slightly incorrect and tinged with an Eastern European accent.

"Nope," Sheila shrugged, "I'm just standing here wondering what to do with an extra fecking second."

"What?" a confused voice shot back, "I don't…."

"Ah, never mind," Sheila continued, taking the gold outfit from the woman's hands, "What happened this time Luana?"

"Sergei, again," the younger woman explained, shaking her head, "He try to catch me and grab my swimsuit instead."

"Leotard Luana, it's a leotard," the fortune-teller corrected, holding the garment up to survey the tear.

"You can fix?"

"Yes, no problem," Sheila sighed, tossing it on to her repair pile, "I'll bring it over later."

With plenty to occupy her time that afternoon, it was six o'clock before Sheila left her caravan to deliver the various items that had required her skill and attention. Firstly surveying the wet and muddy ground outside, she pulled on her rubber boots and mackintosh, no longer looking anything like a fortune-teller but more akin to a middle-aged housewife. Making her way across the field to where a cluster of trailers, caravans and camper vans were situated, Sheila was greeted at every step. It should have only taken quarter of an hour to make her deliveries but such was the activity outside tonight that, after stopping to drink tea with the tent master, chatting to four or five perform-ers along the way and then spending ten minutes watching the fearless motorcycle stuntman practising his new tricks, an hour passed before Sheila had even realised.

"I'd given up on you coming out of your cosy little den tonight," a deep voice called as Sheila carefully made her way back across the field, trying to avoid the puddles, "Thought you might be avoiding me."

She turned, wishing that her outfit wasn't quite so frumpy, and smiled her best smile.

"Good evening Roland. Are you finished for the night?"

"Ah, no chance," the burly man laughed, "Lots still to do before I can turn in for the night. Why, were you going to invite me over for a nightcap Sheila?"

"Don't be silly," she blushed, "You've more chance of the Pope calling in for tea."

The ringmaster thrust his hands deep into his pockets and made to walk away, "You kill me sweetheart," he chuckled, "You really do."

Back in her caravan, tidying away the fabric remnants that she'd used to repair some of the costumes, Sheila smiled to her-self. She'd become quite close to Roland over the past couple of years and it was a wonderful feeling when he paid her atten-tion, although she knew there would be plenty of women he'd have his eye on as soon as the crowds started to arrive the next evening. Sheila had caught sight of a few indiscretions, young ladies leaving the man's caravan in the early hours, and also heard the fiery arguments between Roland and his father that always followed.

By sunlight the next morning, the field had been transformed into the most wondrous hive of activity, with the big top up and coloured flags adorning every guide rope. Curious children from the town had been out early on their bicycles too, hoping to catch a glimpse of the clowns without their painted faces and cheekily daring each other to sneak into the main tent arena to see what was going on inside. The tent master always took great pleasure in chasing the local kids away but he did so in jest, pretending to wave an angry fist as he ran after them at a much slower pace than he would usually give chase. Of course the first night, or opening night, in any new town was always the most exciting for the circus performers. It was the night on which they would gage their audience's reactions, trigger that first barrel of laughter and occasionally do that one off the cuff action that the town would forever remember them for.

In the home of 'Psychic Sheila' the day was all about hiding away her most personal belongings, setting out the tools of her trade such as lace tablecloths and candles and polishing up the most prized possession, her crystal ball. Unlike many traditional Romanies who plied the same trade, Sheila's crystal ball hadn't been handed down to her through the generations, nor had it belonged to a mentor, but quite simply she'd bought it at an antiques auction many years ago. Heavy and shimmering, with an enormous glass globe on the top, the base was made up of a mountain of silver bats, their rat-like faces showing sharp teeth, giving the impression that any sudden movement would cause them to bite. Sheila kept her crystal ball in a metal case, originally designed for carrying photographic equipment and now lined with dark purple velvet padding, a result of her own clever craftsmanship.

"Come to me my lovely," the psychic cooed, carefully taking the item out of its case and wiping the glass surface gently with a soft cloth, "We have work to do tonight."

Sheila leaned over the top of the globe until she could see her own reflection peering back at her. It was at this point on every performance night that plain old Irish-born Sheila Hannigan was transformed into the amazing and talented 'Psychic

Sheila', the wondrous fortune-teller who could see far into the future with her mystic charm and magical crystal ball.

"Bloody hell," she grumbled, looking more closely at her reflection, "I've got lipstick on my teeth! Now there's a bad omen if ever there was one."

Sheila carefully wiped at the red stain on her front tooth with a small piece of tissue and checked herself again in a large vanity mirror on the wall, still not content with the way she looked tonight.

"I'll have to do," she told herself, still frowning, "I can hear the footsteps of paying customers."

Sure enough, a line of young women waited patiently outside. It was always the case, the girls came first, hoping to learn some nugget of insight into their future, while their boyfriends and husbands loitered around waiting to hear the results of their beloved's fifteen minutes inside 'Psychic Sheila's' caravan. Later on in the evening, swallowing their pride or sometimes just simply curious, a few of the males would knock on the door themselves, wanting to hear what fate had in store for them. Sheila always tried to be a little bit more sympathetic to the men who visited, as many were shy and others non-believers, therefore needing gentle persuasion to open up to her. That particular night, it was a pretty blonde woman in her mid-twenties who was first through the door.

"Hello my dear," Sheila smiled, indicating to the chair on the opposite side of the table, "Please sit down."

The woman smiled widely, showing a large gap between her front teeth, "Thank you."

Sheila gently took the blonde's hands in hers and closed her eyes as she found it useful to generate the right atmosphere and helped to clear her mind. She held tight for a few moments and then breathed deeply, pulling her crystal ball towards her as she did so. Those moments of reflection had enabled Sheila to feel a slight ridge on the woman's wedding finger, indicating that a ring had recently been removed. She looked down into the glass orb and glanced up briefly for effect.

"I can see a young man walking away from you," the psychic murmured, "Not so very long ago."

The woman nodded but said nothing.

"It was a serious relationship," Sheila continued, glancing up and noticing her customer's tearful eyes, "But I see something else. I see another man, maybe a year or so in the future. He's tall and handsome, and will make you very happy."

"Will we have children?" the woman asked eagerly, obviously cheered up by the news of her new beau.

"The mist is unclear," Sheila confessed, but then suddenly sensing the other woman's stiffening poise she quickly added, "Yes, my dear, I believe you will."

"Oh, thank you. I never thought I could be happy again without Kevin."

"You will," Sheila smiled, sitting upright again, "Happier than you've ever been."

The young woman opened her purse and took out money to pay, the shoulder pads in her summer dress rustling slightly as she moved. Sheila thought how chic her client looked with additional padding in her frock and vowed to add some to her own clothes when she had a moment free, all thoughts of Kevin gone.

"Do you have a dog?" Sheila asked, tucking the note that the woman offered into her bra, "I sense a small brown puppy."

The young gap-toothed woman beamed, "Yes, his name's Ben. I got him for company a week ago."

Sheila nodded, her senses never failed her, they just sometimes took a while to get going.

"Love him with all your heart," she whispered, "He'll be more loving and faithful than any man."

And so the afternoon continued, with a steady throng of customers trotting in and out of the fortune-teller's caravan, some of the readings being more accurate than others depending upon the vibes between client & medium, until early evening when it was time for Sheila Hannigan to pack away the tools of her trade and venture out to watch the show, as she had done every night for the past five years.

The atmosphere outside the big top was electric with sideshows warming up the crowd and excited children running to and fro pleading with their parents to part with their hard-earned cash for ice-creams, toffee apples and candy floss. The Irishwoman watched as a long queue of circus-goers filed into the main arena, everyone chattering with glee as they showed their tickets and rushed in to find their seats. Sheila pulled her shawl closely around her and walked to the rear of the enormous tent, where the Tent Master was keeping an eye on proceedings.

"Evening Jake," she whispered, catching the man by surprise, "Everything running like clockwork?"

"Oh, Sheila! You'll give me a heart attack one of these days!" the fifty-year old complained jokingly, "All ready, just waiting for your Majesty to take a seat."

It was an in joke with the circus crowd that Jake Collins had a soft spot for Sheila and lately he'd started calling her his 'Princess', much to the woman's annoyance.

Tonight though she was in good spirits, having had a decent amount of money cross her palm, and gave the worker a gentle punch on the arm before brushing past and making her way through the canvas door. Sheila's regular perch was right at the back of the crowd, close to the huge red curtains that shrouded the performers from view while they waited for their turn in the ring, and the rest of the audience didn't give her a second glance without her traditional gipsy costume and red lipstick. It felt empowering to be able to sit amongst the general public while the rest of her circus family performed but Sheila also believed that she could use her powers to protect them from mishaps and sat with baited breath as each act took their turn. As the music began, the woman wiggled herself to the very edge of the seat and awaited the entrance of the ringmaster himself, The Great Rolando.

In actual fact, Roland O'Hare had only been hosting the circus acts for two years. He'd taken over the role when his father had decided to take things more slowly after a mild heart attack, although Roland senior, better known as Roly, still very much held the reins and watched his son's performance with a critical eye. It was the older of the two men who now, quite unexpectedly, sidled along the back row to sit beside Sheila.

"Evening," she said politely, continuing to stare straight ahead.

"Are you alright Sheila?" the man asked gruffly, his Irish accent much more pronounced than her own.

"Yes, I'm fine thanks Roly."

"Look, I know you and I haven't really been close, but I do worry about you being on your own so much and I know for a fact that my Tammy wouldn't want you to be lonely, God rest her soul."

Sheila blinked but still didn't turn to face the man at her side. It had been a few years since Tammy O'Hare had passed away and even though the two women weren't particularly close, they had shared some laughs and their friendship had been steadily growing. At last she found the words to reply.

"Really, you don't need to worry about me. I'm absolutely fine."

"Well, if you're sure," the man grunted, now straining his neck as his son walked into the ring.

"Yes, I am," Sheila told him, although both their attention was now fixed firmly on the younger man.

"Ladies and Gentlemen, welcome to Rolando's Circus! I am 'The Great Rolando' and will be your host for the evening."

The ringmaster stepped forward and took a bow as the crowd clapped and cheered. He look resplendent in his red coat and long leather boots and, looking around at the faces of the women in the audience, Sheila could see that he was making quite an impression on the ladies. She noticed how Roland's muscular arms were stretching the fabric on the seams of his sleeves and gave an involuntary sigh as she predicted that they would need mending within the week.

"Ah, so that's your game is it?" Roland senior tutted, a look of disgust blatant on his face.

"What? No, how could you even think…"

"Don't give me that Missy, I saw the look on your face just now," Roly growled, getting up to leave.

Sheila watched the rest of the show alone. She hadn't known what to make of Roland O'Hare senior's outburst but quite frankly the only thing she cared about was her own reputation. Being a single woman in such a tight knit community was no easy thing but she had hardly expected the older man to be so abrupt with her. Unless of course, he too had designs on her, which she found both a repulsive and odd prospect.

By eleven, the crowds had disappeared, their curiosity satisfied. Performers had retired to their mobile homes to get changed, wash, eat or simply sleep. The few people who still milled about outside were mostly workers who checked on the rigging and tightened the security ropes for the night but even those few men were exhausted and looked forward to settling down.

Sheila lay fully clothed on her bunk, sipping a glass of red wine, and still thinking through the various conversations that had taken place that day, both personal and professional. She hadn't eaten since devouring the bacon sandwich earlier and the effects of the alcohol were making her slightly light-headed. As she clambered off the bed to explore the contents of her tiny fridge there was a tap at the door. At first she ignored it, hoping that the visitor would think she was asleep but then realised that her lights were still on and opened the door. Jake Collins stood in the rain.

"What is it?" she snapped, being unintentionally harsh.

"I just wanted to check you were alright Sheila," Jake countered, the frosty reception going right over his head.

"What the hell's the matter with everyone?" Sheila Hannigan cried, slamming the refrigerator door shut, "Why on earth wouldn't I be alright? And why all the sudden fecking interest?"

The tent master stepped back slightly, unaware of what he'd said wrong.

"Look Sheila, I don't mean to pry, honest I don't," he began timidly, "But when I saw Roly talking to you in the tent this evening, I thought maybe he was making a move on you."

The psychic let out a high-pitched cackle, something which emulated a witch and a sound that led Jake to believe that he'd been mistaken in his observations.

"Would you get out of here Jake Collins!" Sheila chuckled, waving her hands at him, "I've never heard such a ridiculous load of baloney in all my life! Go on now, go on."

The man thrust his hands into the pockets of his worn jeans and turned to leave, glancing back only once.

"I'm sorry Princess," he called, "It's only because I care about you."

"Aye, and every fecker else," Sheila muttered, slamming the caravan door.

That night Sheila Hannigan didn't sleep well at all and the hours in which she did manage to doze off were filled with dreams of her circus family trying to get her married off to one or other of the single men who shared their community. Eventually, at five o'clock in the morning, she drank a strong black coffee and then dressed in jeans and a thick sweater, intending to go for a stroll.

The countryside surrounding the circus campsite was quite breathtaking, and Sheila hadn't really been able to appreciate its full glory upon arrival. Neighbouring fields held flocks of sheep, their white fleeces fluffy like soft marshmallows against the landscape, and the low bleating of a ewe calling her lambs was the only sound to be heard as the woman turned onto a narrow lane. It had rained overnight, not an uncommon thing in Central England, therefore Sheila walked in the middle to avoid deep puddles near the uneven grass verge. She breathed in the fresh air, exhaling slowly through her nose and thinking through both the conversations and strange dreams of the previous night. Sheila made a mental note to apologise to Jake Collins, she knew he just cared about her wellbeing, but why couldn't anyone believe that she could be happy and single in her middle-aged years?

Sheila Hannigan sighed deeply, an action that triggered a bout of coughing and saw her leaning upon a fence post until the irritation passed. She made a quick mental note to cut down on the cigarettes.

"Are you alright?" a familiar husky voice called from behind her.

Sheila turned at the sound of Roland O'Hare's voice, wondering how long he'd been behind her.

"What are you doing here?" she asked, trying to keep the surprise out of her question.

"I'm just taking in the views so I am," the young man smiled, "Bit early for you though isn't it?"

Sheila nodded, another coughing fit starting up, "I couldn't sleep," she eventually managed.

"You want to lay off those fags so you do," Roland lectured, "They do terrible things to your lungs."

"Well, thank you Einstein," Sheila shot back sarcastically, as she recovered herself.

"Come on, will you let me make you a cup of coffee?" the man asked softly, gesturing back towards the tents and caravans behind them, "You look like you need one."

"Alright," the woman conceded, "Although we'll have it at mine."

Roland nodded, linking his arm through hers, "No funny business though, I've got work to do."

Sheila laughed at that comment and looked up into the man's face. He had the same eyes as his father.

"You're a devil Roland O'Hare, that's for sure."

As they approached the cluster of trailers, laughing and chatting, the pair could see that their circus family was beginning to stir. A few items of laundry hung out to dry on a washing-line, two dogs chased each other in circles while their owner drank tea on the step of his caravan and smoke gently curled from the chimney of another as the occupant cooked breakfast. A normal day in circus life, except for one curious action now taking place as the couple approached the main field.

The caravan closest to them was a colourful affair, painted with the stars and stripes of the American flag and emblazoned with images of a daredevil stuntman. It belonged to the newest member of the group, an Evil Knievel look-a-like who defied death on his custom-built motorbike. He stood outside the door of his mobile home at that very moment, stretching and yawning before picking up a very dainty red watering-can.

Sheila nudged Roland and giggled, "What's he up to?"

"Looks like Danger McDougall's got green fingers."

"Well, I don't see any fecking flowers, do you?" his companion laughed, "Oh sorry Roland, there I go again, swearing, I'll have to wash my mouth out with soap."

"You will my girl," he scorned, "Far too much swearing! Now what's he up to?"

"Maybe he's got a few pot plants, that's all. Now are we having that coffee or what?"

The young man sighed & nodded, "We are, I'll race you to the kettle."

Chapter Two

Danger McDougall

A while later, after an hour or so waking up the rest of the crew by tearing around on his motorbike, Danger McDougall had occasion to knock at Sheila Hannigan's door. This was by no means an unusual occurrence, as you can imagine, as the stuntman regularly had mishaps where he accidentally tore up his overalls, jeans and leather jackets, but on this particular day it was an all-in-one jumpsuit that he carried to the psychic's caravan.

Sheila had just finished hand-washing some underwear and opened her door just as the man approached.

"Oh, hello," she chirped, a little startled, "Were you after my services?"

"Morning," the stunt rider smiled back, "Could I be cheeky and ask you to sew some of the lettering back onto my suit please? The stitching's coming undone."

"No problem at all," Sheila quipped, "Just drop it on my work table inside, I need to peg my washing out."

Danger McDougall blushed as he glanced down at the lacy knickers in Sheila's hand and then quickly stepped inside her home to deposit his jumpsuit as directed.

Standing six feet tall, and strongly built, Sheila had to look up to her visitor as he departed. She stood on the damp grass, pegging out her washing and was almost a foot shorter.

"Will you be needing that done for tonight?" she asked, mentally counting the other tasks she needed to see to before customers would start to arrive.

"I'm doing a ring of fire display at five," the man told her, "Is that okay?"

Sheila simply lifted her chin in acknowledgement and continued her chore.

"I'll pop back for it about half four," Mr. McDougall called, raising his hand to smooth down his sleek black hair as he walked away, "And thanks again, much appreciated."

Sheila watched him out of the corner of her eye, "He's a strange one," she tutted, "Scottish name, a van covered in the American flag, a Merseyside accent and he dresses up like Elvis! Lord help us!"

But it wasn't the origins of his name, his background or his mother-tongue that intrigued Sheila Hannigan, no, it was the way in which the daredevil rider limped away to his trailer, every step looking more painful than the next, something which she hadn't noticed him doing the evening before.

As promised, just before four-thirty, Danger McDougall tapped on the door of 'Psychic Sheila's' caravan.

"Here you go," a very glamorous-looking Sheila announced, holding up the jumpsuit for inspection, "I've double-stitched the letters, so they should last you a good while."

"Ah, thanks very much Sheel, that's brill," the stuntman grinned as he checked out the stitching.

"Sheila," the gipsy woman corrected, "Not Sheel, Shell, Eela, or anything else, just Sheila."

"Sorry," Mr. McDougall apologised, hanging his head slightly, "That's a bad habit of mine."

"It's ok, I'm just teasing," Sheila chuckled, trying to lighten the mood, "I just don't like it being shortened."

"Anyway, look, thanks for this," the stuntman offered, holding up his outfit, "If ever you need anything…."

"No problem, I'll come and watch your set if I don't have many customers."

Sheila closed the door slowly, watching the tall man walk away. He was no longer limping.

Psychic Sheila was busy that night, not finishing her readings until eight o'clock, by which time Danger McDougall's opening stunt ride had been over for a couple of hours. There was still time to watch the second half of the performance in the main tent though and as she lifted the canvas to sneak inside, a loud roar went up in the audience, caused by the agile antics of the Russian acrobats. Sheila climbed to the back tiered row, carefully trying to avoid candy floss sticking to her clothing as she passed a group of small children waving their sugary sticks around in excitement. She soon spotted Roland's father sitting alone next to an empty seat, the one which was usually hers, but climbed on regardless.

"So there you are," Roly O'Hare mused, eyeing the psychic closely as she arrived, "You've been busy tonight."

"Look, I don't know what's been going through that mind of yours…" Sheila began.

"Ah, come on, I'm trying to be nice," the older man grinned, "I'm sorry for what I said last night. You and I both know that my son is far too young for you don't we?"

Sheila didn't know if the comment was a warning or a statement but turned to look the Irishman in the eye regardless. "Yes, we do," she hissed, "And I would never ever be interested anyway."

The circus show was electrifying that evening, everyone performed to their best ability, the crowd were responsive at all the right times and laughter filled the air. Both the acts and the audience exited the Big Top feeling elated, while at the back of the tent Sheila Hannigan fumed.

Roly O'Hare had departed about half an hour before the end of the show, leaving Sheila to think about his comments alone. It was obvious that the old man saw her as some kind of man-eating phenomenon who intended to lure away his one and only son and his accusing tone made the younger woman feel miserable. She wouldn't have minded so much if she really did have dishonorable intentions towards Roland but the fact was, despite her great fondness towards him, Sheila Hannigan would never so much as accept a kiss from him. What she had to do now was keep some distance between them until the lad's father came to his senses.

"Are you intending sitting up here all night?"

Sheila had been so caught up in her own thoughts that she hadn't noticed the Elvis Presley look-alike coming to sit at her side, although she immediately recognised the white sparkly jumpsuit.

"Mr. McDougall," she smiled, at once recovering, "No, I was just thinking about going to my van."

"Would you like to join me for a bite to eat? I make a mean cheese on toast."

Sheila shook her head, she worried far too much what others might think if she entered a man's home by herself, "I don't think so, but thank you for offering."

"I erm, have an ulterior motive," McDougall confessed, turning to show her his sleeve, "I seem to have burnt my suit on the flames tonight."

Sheila put a hand on the fabric to see if it had melted all the way through, "It's not too bad, I can repair that in no time at all."

"In the time it takes for me to make cheese on toast?" the stuntman asked cheekily, raising an eyebrow to tempt her, "I've got Cornetto ice-creams for dessert."

Sheila grabbed her shawl and stood up, "Now you're talking, give me five minutes to get my sewing box."

Danger McDougall led the way outside, "I'll go and make a start on supper," he said.

The accident had happened at the end of his performance that evening. With wind speed increasing and the flaming hoops being lightweight, it hadn't taken much for the stuntman to misjudge where he needed to leap and, adding the light frame of the motorcycle into the mix, had veered too far to the right, causing the edge of his jumpsuit to catch fire. The flames had been put out almost immediately, the safety team were good at that, but it still left Danger McDougall's suit in rather a sorry state.

"I think I might have to be creative with this," Sheila confessed after looking closely at the singed fabric, "What if I put some patches either side to make it look like intentional decoration?"

"Aw, thanks. Thought I might have to fork out for a new one for a minute."

"You will if you carry on!" Sheila joked, threading a needle, "Do you have many accidents?"

The young man turned from where he'd been making a brew and shrugged, his face honest and open.

"My name's 'Danger' isn't it? Wouldn't be right if I didn't have a few tumbles."

"I noticed you limping earlier…" Sheila started.

"Oh, that. Comes and goes, nothing but a bit of arthritis."

"At your age? Surely not," Sheila replied, wondering if she sounded as though she were prying.

Danger McDougall laughed, "Do you like brown sauce on your cheese?"

Sheila could spot a conversation diversion a mile off and answered in the affirmative before getting back to her needlework. She sincerely hoped that she hadn't offended.

After supper, of which the toast was too crisp and the cheese too sparse, the pair sat on the bunks eating their chocolate cones and watching 'The Twilight Zone' on McDougall's portable black and white television.

"It's nice to have a bit of company," the Merseysider commented, his gaze still focused on the screen.

"Yes, it is," Sheila agreed, squinting as she struggled to see the action without her spectacles.

"We should do this again sometime," the stuntman said casually, still unmoving.

Sheila stiffened, but then, after a few seconds, relaxed a little, "Yes why not."

The following day was wet and cold. A thick blanket of fog had settled upon the showground overnight and the few workers who were up and about early were wrapped up in thick overcoats and woollen hats. Sheila wasn't an early riser by nature, preferring to rouse herself slowly, with firstly a cup of coffee in bed, then a cigarette as she took in some fresh air at her caravan doorway, before finally showering and pulling on some clothes. That particular morning, however, Sheila had no intention of letting the cold, crisp winter air drift inside and instead lay huddled beneath her quilted eiderdown with the curtain pulled back slightly, allowing just enough vision to peruse the comings and goings outside.

She could make out the tall figure of Roly O'Hare, striding across to the main tent in his heavy donkey jacket, he walked with a slight stoop of the shoulders, hands stuffed deeply into his pockets, a man very obviously deep in thought. To the right of the Big Top stood Danger McDougall's trailer and, casting her eyes upon it now, Sheila could see the stuntman suddenly emerging with something red in his hands. Her eyes weren't sharp enough to see the object with clarity, therefore quickly rummaging about to locate them, Sheila Hannigan popped her spectacles on and peered out.

"Well damn me," she mumbled, "He's out with his little watering-can again."

Now like a spy on a top-secret mission, the gipsy woman dressed in record time, even foregoing her second dawn cigarette and wrapped up against the freezing elements. She headed straight for the daredevil's home, with a cup of steaming coffee in each hand, under the guise that she had simply brought over a little something to warm her friend through. As she approached, Danger McDougall was nowhere to be seen and Sheila feared that she had been too slow to catch him outdoors but suddenly there was a groan from underneath the trailer and the six-foot hunk slid out.

"Well, what on earth are you doing under there?" the woman exclaimed, almost spilling the hot drinks.

"Sheila!" her friend gulped, his eyes wide like a rabbit caught in headlights, "I was just erm…"

"What? What were you doing underneath your caravan at six o'clock in the morning?"

Danger McDougall glanced down and realised that he still held the red watering-can in his hand.

"I was just putting some oil on the axel," he explained, "It's been squeaking lately."

"Why don't you get yourself an oil can then, like any normal man?" Sheila laughed, "If anyone catches you with that little thing they'll think you're a poof."

The stuntman laughed and set the small can down on the step, "Come on in, I'll make breakfast."

Sheila passed the cups of coffee up to her friend and put a foot on the caravan step but hesitated before going inside. She glanced upwards to ensure that her companion was preoccupied and then quickly bent down to touch the watering-can, dipping a finger inside to check the contents. It was water.

As they sat eating crispy bacon and watery scrambled eggs, Danger McDougall kept the conversation flowing with his plans to add some new and more daring stunts to his evening routine. So excited was he with sharing the ideas that he failed to notice the Irishwoman's silence. Sheila was a polite guest, and nodded appropriately as the man talked animatedly but all the time she was in deep thought about the lack of oil in Danger McDougall's can. It was a strange and insignificant thing to ponder but once Sheila had a mystery on her hands, there was no reasoning with her until it was solved.

"I think I might add an extra ring of fire this summer," her companion was saying, "What do you think?"

Sheila didn't respond, but her fork moved scrambled egg around the plate as she continued to brood.

"Sheila? Am I boring you?" the stuntman laughed, "Or is it my terrible cooking?"

"Mmm? Oh, I'm sorry, it's still a bit early for me," the woman managed, pushing aside her breakfast, "What were you saying?"

"Never mind," came the response, "Just come and watch me later. Deal?"

Sheila agreed and got up to leave, carefully stepping onto the wet grass in her sensible shoes, and paused to pick up the little red can.

"Don't forget this," she winked, as her friend followed her to the door. And then, in a moment of devilment, Sheila tipped the contents out onto the grass and grinned, "You can't oil an axel with water."

Danger McDougall stood open-mouthed, trying desperately to come up with a response. Nothing.

"See you later," the woman quipped, skipping back across the grass to her caravan, satisfaction written upon her face at the embarrassment she had just caused.

Two trailers along, Roland O'Hare the younger was just opening his curtains and immediately noticed the stuntman watching a very happy Sheila Hannigan as she picked her way back across the field.

That afternoon the dismal weather continued, although the fog did lift slightly and the rain went from torrential to an icy drizzle but it was enough to significantly reduce the number of customers at 'Psychic Sheila's' door and by four o'clock she hadn't done a single reading. The Irishwoman tapped her long nails nervously on the table and then lit a cigarette. She couldn't decide whether to venture out in her raincoat to watch the daredevil motorcyclist or just to sit and keep warm inside her cosy home. A decision could only be made by reaching for the television switch, if there was a good film showing, Sheila would stay indoors, if not she'd wrap up and go to the display. It took a few moments for the screen to stop flickering as the portable television burst into life but immediately the shrill voices of the 'Golden Girls' could be heard as they acted out another episode of the daytime show.

"That settles it then," the psychic grumbled as she reached for her knitted scarf, "I'm not watching that."

Over at the display arena, a small crowd of youngsters had gathered to watch Danger McDougall leap through an enormous hoop, which was balanced on top of a specially made platform with a ramp running up to it. The hoop had been doused in petrol and, as Sheila approached, one of the regular circus workers prepared to light it. Naturally, due to the pouring rain, it took several attempts for the fire to ignite properly and as the flames leapt slowly upwards, a murmur went through the onlookers.

Danger McDougall was circling the arena, the engine of his lightweight scrambler bike revving as the throttle was pulled back and forth, the rider himself checking that everything was perfect before positioning himself for the final jump. Despite having done this very same performance hundreds of times over, the stuntman never took his luck for granted and touched the shiny Saint Christopher pendant around his neck for good luck, before spinning off in one last lap for the crowd's pleasure. Then, as the flames rose higher, the daredevil rider took his post at the end of the ramp and pushed his stead forth in a surge of speed and adrenalin. Nobody breathed, the atmosphere was tense until Danger McDougall reached the other side, unburnt by the fire and still safely astride his beloved motorcycle.

That was until he reached the sodden grass on the other side, tyres skidding in the mud the whole front end of the bike sliding out from under its rider. The stuntman tumbled across the arena, his legs doing cartwheels in the air as he glided along, and loud shrieks came surging forth from the onlookers. Sheila was running, trying desperately to keep her eyes upon her friend but trying to avoid the jostling crowd who were moving towards the edge of the stadium. Suddenly, as she reached a point where the stuntman could be seen clearly, he stood up and took off his helmet, one arm sweeping low as he took a bow. Sheila sucked in her breath and slowed down her pace to a walk, cursing the man's foolishness as she went.

"Danger Mc Feckin' Dougall," the psychic exclaimed as she approached the group of circus workers who were checking the stuntman for damage, "I nearly had a heart attack."

The man turned to face her, laughter creasing the corners of his mouth, "Convincing wasn't it?"

Sheila punched him on the arm and cursed again, "Don't you dare tell me you did that on purpose! Why would you even do that?"

"Actually, no I didn't," the young man confessed, "But the fans don't know that do they?"

Sheila Hannigan shook her head, a few loose dark curls escaping from the hood of her raincoat, "You're a damned fool, so you are. Daredevil stuntman my arse, you're a fecking lunatic."

As she stomped back to her caravan, Sheila was unaware of another set of eyes watching the scene.

That evening, having consumed a couple of egg mayonnaise sandwiches and several cups of tea, Sheila prepared to go back outside. It was half an hour before the Circus performances would begin in the Big Top and already she could hear the beat of Jennifer Rush's 'Power of Love' booming out through the loudspeakers, enticing the locals to abandon their warm homes in exchange for an evening's entertainment. Suddenly there was a tap at the door.

"There she is, the heartbreaker herself," Roland O'Hare exclaimed as he climbed inside, "Any more tea in the pot Sheila?"

"What are you doing here?" she exclaimed, looking the handsome ringmaster up and down. He looked rather dashing in his costume but Sheila's first instinct was to survey him for rips and tears, "Is it my sewing skills you're after Roland?"

"Not at all," the gent smiled, showing his perfect white teeth, "I just came to see how you are. Getting a bit friendly with our resident biker aren't you Sheila?"

"Well, what if I am?" she returned haughtily, "He seems a decent chap."

Roland reached for a grape from the fruit bowl on the table, "Just watch it doesn't turn sour sweetheart."

The psychic puffed her cheeks out and put her hands on her hips, "What are you trying to say?"

"Nothing Sheila," he grinned, turning to leave, "Nothing at all, sweetheart."

That night was the first in five years that Sheila Hannigan didn't watch the performers. Naturally she was missed by her fellow circus family members but there were several reasons that she needed time alone. The Irish woman's friendship with Danger McDougall had started off quite well, considering they hadn't really engaged in a proper conversation since his arrival two years previously, and she was in awe at how dangerous his stunts really were, but no level of understanding could help her to comprehend the reaction of Roland O'Hare. Sheila lay back on her bunk, sucking heavily on yet another cigarette, and mulled over the events of the past few days. She neither wanted nor needed any complication in her life, after all nobody knew the real Sheila Hannigan, and vowed to consign herself to a life of spinsterhood to avoid all misunderstanding. That night she dreamed heavily, of handsome men, angry old ones and her own difficult Catholic father who, very oddly, just happened to be carrying a little red watering-can.

Standing with a cigarette poised between her fingers the next morning, Sheila lifted her face upwards to the sun and said a silent prayer for the change in weather conditions. Today was to be the last on this particular site and a large crowd was predicted for the finale, as tomorrow would see the travelling show parade back through the town and head off in an entirely new direction. It would soon be Easter and the fortune-teller wondered whether the next town might have a Catholic church which she could visit but, if not, Sheila would settle for her rosary beads and a few days of minding her P's and Q's.

As her lids fluttered open, Sheila Hannigan noticed a certain stunt rider emerging from underneath his trailer, a familiar red object clutched in his hand. The hunk was too busy concentrating on not slipping over to notice the woman watching and furtively brushed down his jeans as he stood upright. Even without her glasses, Sheila could see that the man had been 'oiling his axel' again. How puzzling, she mused.

Continuing to stand in the caravan doorway, the psychic reached for her coffee, which had already started to cool, and turned her thoughts to more mundane tasks, such as polishing her brass ornaments and preparing for the afternoon's clientele. It was going to be a long day, she could feel it in her bones, but something much more serious than housework was just about to happen.

The shouts came at five o'clock, just as 'Psychic Sheila's' last customer was preparing to leave. It had been a fairly straightforward reading, another young woman excited to learn whether a tall, dark and handsome man was just around the corner. The gipsy woman had told the truth, as much as she could fathom from the swirling colours in her crystal ball, and then suddenly a bright orange glow from the glass orb had almost knocked her backwards in alarm.

"Something 's going to happen," Sheila exclaimed, her eyes wide in fear.

"To me?" the young red-head seated at the table cried, "What did you see?"

"No love, not you, someone else. Sorry, get your coat, I've got to go."

The customer dropped a couple of notes on the table and pulled on her jacket, "Thanks again Sheila, see you next year hopefully, have a good summer."

Sheila nodded gratefully and ushered the twenty-year old out through the door, grabbing her own coat and putting a key in the lock as she did so, "You're very welcome Juliette, see you next year."

Racing across the grass, Sheila instinctively knew exactly where to head for, the motorbike stunt arena.

Already a large group of circus workers had gathered, blocking her view of the scene but, by pushing to the front of the crowd, Sheila could see the prostrate figure of Danger McDougall lying on the ground. Her heart felt as though it stopped completely for a few seconds as Sheila stood looking down at the unmoving body, but instinct took over and she reached down to lift up the visor on her friend's helmet.

"Can you hear me?" she whispered softly, "Please God be alive."

Danger McDougall's eyes shot open at the sound of the gentle Irish voice at his side, "I'm alright, I think, although I can't move my left leg."

"An ambulance is on its way son," Roly O'Hare announced from behind Sheila's shoulder, "That'll teach you to do one too many wheelies now so it will."

The stuntman smiled, wincing as pain shot up his broken leg but he didn't take his eyes off Sheila, who rode with him to the hospital and waited there until the next morning when he was finally released. The man had been lucky, an easy break to reset and his leg in a plaster cast for a couple of months, both he and the crew knew it could have been much worse.

Arriving back at the campsite by taxi the following morning, everyone was packing up and dismantling the tents ready to hit the road the following day. The entire circus family stopped to cheer as Danger McDougall and his chaperone alighted from the mini bus, causing a great deal of embarrassment to Sheila in her dishevelled state but pure delight for the patient.

"Come on, let's get you inside your van," the woman cursed, "Then I need a hot shower."

"Will you not stay with me for a while?" Danger McDougall pouted, pretending he was upset as he balanced precariously on his wooden crutches.

"No," she insisted, "I look like a cat who's been caught out in a snowstorm! I'll be back later."

With only minimal packing to do in preparation for the next day's journey, Sheila spent some time preparing food and making herself look more presentable. Her back ached from sleeping in a hospital chair and the clothes that she'd been wearing were crumpled and sweaty. Within an hour and a half, the psychic felt back to her old self and made her way back over to the stuntman's caravan, bearing a pan of beef broth and wearing a floaty blue dress.

"Hiya," Danger McDougall grinned, as he lay with his injured leg on a bunk, "What have you got there?"

Sheila lifted the saucepan lid, letting the aroma drift across the room, "Beef broth and dumplings."

Her friend sniffed appreciatively but then winced as a twinge of pain travelled up his leg, "You'll make someone a grand wife one day Sheila, you mark my words."

Sheila pretended not to hear and opened a cupboard in search of bowls.

The break in the stuntman's leg wasn't the first in his career, and the young man seemed to be managing to get around fairly well over the next few days as the entourage headed south. He'd travelled inside Sheila's caravan with her for company, lounging back on her multitude of cushions, and the pair had passed the time playing cards and Scrabble. Every time they stopped at a petrol station or café, it had been Sergei Chekov, the Russian acrobat, who had raced over to see if any assistance was needed in getting to the lavatory or fetching provisions but rarely did the couple venture out from their hideaway until the circus finally arrived in the West Midlands.

Hobbling back to his own trailer, which had now been unhitched from the vehicle towing it and hooked up to the power, Danger McDougall threw back his head in laughter.

"I'm not telling you!" he insisted, "So you might as well stop asking."

"Come on," teased Sheila, who had been niggling at him for the last hour, "You must have a proper name. I can't carry on calling you Danger, is it something really posh like Clarence or Cedric?"

The stuntman shook his head and swung his crutches forward, "Never, in a million years."

Suddenly he stopped, a serious expression appearing on his face, and he turned towards Sheila.

"I need your help with something," he whispered, motioning her to come closer.

Sheila stopped laughing and took a step forward, "Of course, what is it?"

Having now reached his trailer and unlocked it, the stuntman reached inside for the watering-can.

Sheila stood frowning, she was beyond puzzled.

"What am I supposed to do with that?" she blurted, causing a passing worker to turn and look.

"Sshh," Danger McDougall warned, "I need you to feed my plants for me Sheila, they're all racked up on a metal tray, attached to the suspension. They'll die if they don't get watered."

Sheila frowned, "Why can't you put them in window boxes like any normal fecker?"

The hunk rolled his eyes and then realised that she really didn't have a clue. Oh, innocent Sheila.

"They're medicinal herbs," he confessed, ensuring that nobody could overhear, "You don't think I could have so many accidents without something for the pain, do you?"

"What…do you mean…they're cannabis plants?!" the psychic hissed, her eyes wide in excitement.

"Yes," came the reply, "And it's going to be our little secret."

Chapter Three

The Chekovs

Sheila Hannigan had a spring in her step, as did the rest of the circus. It was Easter Bank Holiday weekend and the weather was unusually warm, causing dark moods to lift and smiles to appear as the promise of summer was not so many months away now. It was also an incredibly busy weekend for the performers, with double shows every day, both afternoon and evening, meaning less time to practice and more hours putting on their various costumes and theatrical make-up. For a few weeks now the travellers had moved around middle England and now, for their grand finale, they set up camp close to the city centre. For Sheila it meant the return of many old customers and of course a hoard of new followers too, keeping her busy for many hours across the weekend.

The journey to the city had been short and uneventful. Sheila was now in the habit of sharing her ride with Danger McDougall, and the pair had spent this trip playing cards and drinking coffee, It was just a platonic friendship, they insisted, but one which filled a gap in both their lives. The stuntman's leg had healed well and this weekend would be his first performance since the accident. As for his unusual plant-watering request, well, the psychic had gone along with it for her friend's sake, being careful to only crawl under Mr.McDougall's trailer late at night in order to tend to his plants and never revealing his secret. In return the daredevil had invited Sheila over to watch his video collection on many occasions and often treated her to a fish and chip supper. All in all, the arrangement was an extremely amicable one.

On Good Friday morning, with the huge red and white striped tent erected and workers rushing to and fro in the course of their duties, the circus family exuded an air of excitement and fun. The clowns were outside, tumbling around and chasing each other as they perfected their intentional clumsiness, causing Roly O'Hare to curse as he tried to pass, while the resident strongman grunted and groaned as he heaved a set of enormous weights onto his muscular shoulders.

Sheila Hannigan instinctively knew that her clients would start arriving around two o'clock, she was psychic after all, which meant a few hours of freedom before having to create her other persona. There were very few tasks which needed attending to in her spotless home and the afternoon's outfit had already been picked out, leaving the woman sitting listening to Elton John on her old and trusty cassette player. Sheila had left the caravan door wide open and a fresh breeze blew gently across her face as she reached in a drawer for a snack. The first thing to touch her fingers was a chocolate Curlywurly bar and it took a mere hesitation of three minutes before the gipsy gave in to temptation and ripped off the wrapper.

There came a sudden knock at the door.

Sheila stuffed the chocolate bar under a cushion and hurriedly checked her face in the mirror for any traces of evidence. Seeing nothing to give away her moment of weakness, she called the visitor to enter.

"Well Luana," she sighed, smiling widely as the petite blonde Russian came through the entry, "How are you this morning?"

"Hello Sheila, I good thanks," the woman replied, her accent heavy and stilted, "Again I need help, I buy some crystal for my costume, I need you sew please."

The Russian held out her hands, in one a dark blue glittery leotard and in the other a pack of diamante beads. Walking over to Sheila's table, she lay down the outfit and began dotting the sparkly objects along the neckline to show the older woman how she would like them to be stitched.

"Is ok?" Luana asked, stepping back to allow Sheila to inspect the garment, "I sorry I always ask."

Sheila Hannigan put her hand on the acrobat's shoulder and rubbed her fingers back and forth, "Don't be silly, you know I don't mind doing it for you."

The contact with Luana Chekov's bare flesh peeking out from her strappy top, suddenly sparked something inside the psychic's mind and she withdrew her hand almost immediately. It was like a mild electric shock and to Sheila that meant the young woman was hiding something.

"Is everything alright Luana?" she asked gently, "You know, if you need someone to talk to I'm here."

The Russian frowned and straightened her back, "I fine, why you ask me?"

"No reason," Sheila sighed, "Just checking. Now, let me see what we can do with this costume of yours. Shall I bring it over in an hour or so?"

"No, no, I come back at six," the young woman insisted, holding up a hand, "Sergei, he take a nap, not to be disturb. I use this suit for evening show. Oh, Sheila, you have chocolate on your teeth."

Sheila watched the agile youngster jump down the step and cartwheel across the grass outside, bewildered as to why she had such a strange sensation upon touching Luana's skin. Could it be that the woman was scared of her husband? Was Sergei a control freak? Mind racing, the gipsy tried to think of a single occasion when she'd seen someone enter the Chekovs caravan. There wasn't one.

As Sheila patiently stitched the crystal beads onto Luana's outfit, her mind worked over-time, trying to recall the last time she had returned a garment to the Chekovs caravan. It hadn't been long ago, she was certain, only a few weeks in fact, and the door to the Russian's home had been closed. Thinking through the scenario now, Sheila was certain that she had heard a bolt being drawn across before Luana had opened the door and greeted her. There had been no invitation to step inside for a moment, just a huge thank you and the door closing once again. It was very strange.

The afternoon, as expected, saw a long queue of customers waiting to see 'Psychic Sheila'. Some were older members of the general public who had recently lost loved ones and the gipsy could sense that their real need was to know that the dearly departed relative was happy on the other side. She was delighted to help in consoling people but Sheila's true enjoyment came from the unexpected predictions that introduced themselves as a flurry of shapes seen in her crystal ball. That day she saw newborn babies, arguing spouses, a brand new red car and somebody hiding money in an old tin box.

As the time for the fortune-teller to close her door for the day, she began to let her mind wander back to the young acrobats who would still be performing in the main tent.

"I'll get to the bottom of this if it kills me," Sheila muttered to herself as she carefully packed away the heavy crystal ball and Tarot cards.

Sure enough, as Sheila's little carriage clock chimed six, Luana Chekov returned to pick up her newly stitched leotard. The woman was still flushed from her strenuous high-flying afternoon performance and beads of sweat clung to her forehead.

"Sheila, you make it fantastic!" she squealed, grinning from ear to ear, "I go show Sergei now."

"Luana, love," Sheila began, thinking quickly, "Would you like me to make you a headband to go with it? There are a few beads left and I've got a piece of fabric that will match."

"Really?" Luana Chekov gasped, unable to control her excitement, "You do it for me?"

"Yes, no problem," the gipsy promised, "I'll run something up for you later."

As the acrobat left, Sheila stood plotting with a cheeky grin on her face.

'Earthquake in Mexico kills thousands' the news reel read at the bottom of Sheila's television screen as she switched it on. The broadcaster had a solemn expression on his face and shuffled a few papers.

"More bad news," Sheila tutted, watching closely as the story unfolded, "Those poor people."

Standing transfixed for a few minutes, watching the scenes of devastation, she pressed the 'OFF' button and picked up the shimmering headband that she'd just spent the last hour making. It was stretchy and sparkly, perfect for a high-flying acrobat. Sheila opened the door in search of Luana.

It took just a few seconds to spot the Russian woman flick-flacking across the grass as she practiced her backward hand-springs for the evening performance. Sheila waved as she approached.

"Hello love, don't stop on my account, I can pop this into your caravan for you," she called as Luana abruptly came to a halt and looked over.

"No, no!" she returned, looking somewhat panic-stricken, "I take."

'Suit yourself dear,' Sheila shrugged, handing the item over, "I hope you like it."

"Sorry, sorry," the youngster apologised catching her friend's arm, "It just Sergei, he inside cooking."

"Well, if you can get your man to cook you a decent meal, he shouldn't be disturbed."

Luana nodded, and pulled the headband on, "Beautiful, it perfect Sheila."

The fortune-teller smiled and continued on to the outdoor arena where Danger McDougall was impressing the last of the afternoon stragglers with his wheelies. Sheila was deep in thought and stood watching but not really taking in the spectacular efforts of her daredevil friend. All concentration was on the Chekovs.

That evening, sitting in her usual spot at the back of the Big Top, Sheila Hannigan vowed to watch the Russian acrobats more closely than ever before as they shocked the crowd with their acrobatics. The tent was filled to maximum capacity, the audience excited not only about the show but the fact that it was a public holiday and many had a few days off to look forward to. Children waved their candy floss and sticky toffee apples as they laughed and giggled at the clowns performing their warm up act, while behind the scenes 'The Great Rolando' gave a last minute pep talk to the other artists. Sheila looked around for Roly O'Hare and glimpsed his familiar donkey jacket moving around at the side of the curtain. He really was a man who couldn't let others get on with their work, she thought.

The Chekovs were the third act to perform that evening, following the strongman and magician. As they bounced into the ring and waited momentarily for a net to be rapidly constructed for their safety, Sheila adjusted her glasses and leaned forward, determined to spot any chinks in their relationship. The performance lasted for fifteen minutes, with the couple gliding through the air at set intervals, gripping the crowd with their incredible feats and daring routine. Luana seemed to have total faith that her husband would catch her every time she let go of the trapeze, and he did, every single time. Sergei was highly skilled in walking the tight-rope too, doing so with poise and elegance as his partner waited on the ground below, her face lit up with pride.

Sheila sat mesmerized. They really were very good, quite possibly the best acrobats in the country but she still couldn't shake that nagging feeling that there was something untoward. Besides, her psychic instincts were rarely wrong and there had most definitely been a surge of energy warning her of something when she'd touched Luana Chekov's arm. She did one last scan as the trapeze artists left the ring, bowing to the crowd as cheers rose and hands clapped, but could not spot a single flaw.

The following day was even sunnier than the previous one and the temperature rose a few degrees. Many of the circus men had stripped down to their vests as they toiled at their various tasks and, peeping out through her net curtains, Sheila Hannigan was quite enjoying the view. Due to the nature of their work, most of the workers were muscular and tanned, a factor that gave the fortune-teller much satisfaction as she admired the toned torsos over a cup of black coffee that morning.

Sheila hadn't slept particularly well, instead tossing and turning as she pondered about her Russian comrades. She wondered if talking through the dilemma with Danger McDougall or Roland might help, but more than likely they'd make jest of her psychic intuition and accuse her of poking her nose into other people's business. No, Sheila decided, she would work this particular issue out all by herself. Just as she was stubbing out her cigarette and swilling around the dregs of her coffee, the gipsy noticed that Luana was now outdoors hanging out some washing. The young woman was dressed in a t-shirt and cotton shorts, revealing something that had been hidden under her sparkly tights the night before, a huge purple bruise.

"Oh hell," Sheila cursed, sucking in her breath, "That damn Sergei's been beating her."

Oblivious to the spectator, Luana gathered up her washing-basket and opened the caravan door to go back inside, the dark mark on her thigh quite large and prominent.

Sheila had a very busy Saturday. At one point she was so concerned that she wouldn't be able to fulfill all of the readings that she almost put up her 'CLOSED' sign at three o'clock. However, her mind flowed easily and everyone went away satisfied, either learning of a new love, hearing about an unexpected inheritance or given a warning not to act irresponsibly. A very productive day for 'Psychic Sheila' but it did mean that it was five o'clock before she was finished and had been unable to drop in on any of her friends that day. After a quick shower and a Pot Noodle to sustain her energy levels, Sheila pulled a pair of jeans and a tennis jumper out of the cupboard and quickly dressed. She wanted to catch Sergei before the evening show.

Strolling casually across the field, Sheila Hannigan keep her eyes fixed on the caravan belonging to the Russian acrobats. Somehow she would need to have a word in the husband's ear, she thought. However, Sheila's tete-a-tete couldn't be executed at that moment as, finding out for herself as she approached, the squeak of bedsprings could be heard quite distinctly coming from inside. Sheila blushed and diverted her path towards the Big Top.

It was empty, as the evening show wasn't due to start until seven o'clock but behind the huge curtain somebody was moving things around. Sheila stepped inside and tugged at the canvas screen that usually separated the audience from showmen, revealing Jake Collins as she did so.

"Hey there Princess," he greeted with a huge smile, "Were you looking for me?"

"No, not exactly Jake," she admitted, immediately noticing the disappointment on the tent master's face, "But I'm very happy to see you."

"You little fibber," Jake teased, continuing to drag a bench along the sawdust floor, "What are you up to?"

"Is it that obvious?" Sheila questioned, raising an eyebrow and folding both arms across her ample bosom.

"Yes, it is," the man laughed, "If you're looking for Roland he's away to get changed."

The comment was like a red rag to a bull and Sheila felt herself growing hot inside. She didn't want to rise to the bait but was fed up to the back teeth of people presuming there was something going on between her and Roland O'Hare. Puffing out her cheeks and exhaling slowly, Sheila picked her words carefully.

"Jake," she began, "As much I as I think you're a lovely man, you don't have as much as an ounce of common sense between those two ears of yours." With that, Sheila stormed off.

Sneaking back past the Chekovs trailer, a natural route on the way to her own of course, she stopped for a moment to catch her breath. A male voice could be heard coming from inside the acrobat's home and the accent was most definitely English.

"Come on LuLu, we've got time for another quickie. Or don't you love me anymore?"

Sheila gasped as she heard the sound of Luana giggling, followed by some very amorous kissing sounds.

"Oh my word," she gasped, rushing quickly home, "The silly girl's having an affair, no wonder Sergei has been giving her a good hiding."

Back within the confines of her caravan, Sheila reached for a bottle of red wine. She promised herself just one glass to steady her fraying nerves while deciding what to do. As she saw it there were three options: she could either warn Luana to end the affair, find out who the other man was and warn him or keep her nose out of it altogether. Telling Sergei was not an alternative, she'd read in one of her women's magazines that Eastern European men could be head-strong and unpredictable. And thinking about predictions, this was one situation that Sheila really had no inkling about. She reached for the bottle and poured another glass, just to steady her nerves of course.

Tap, tap, tap.

Sheila Hannigan opened one eye and glanced at the little carriage clock. She couldn't make out the numerals without her glasses and the turntable was twisting to and fro making her feel dizzy. but it wasn't half as annoying as the persistent tapping at the door.

"Go away," she called, her voice feeble and slurred, "I'm not taking visitors this afternoon."

Much to the woman's horror, the door swung back on its hinges and a muscular man entered.

"What's going on Sheila?" Roland O'Hare asked, genuinely concerned, "Are you alright love?"

Sheila sat up abruptly, hitting her head on the shelf above the bed, "Get out!"

"Well excuse me for caring," the ringmaster laughed, "We were all worried about you darlin'."

"Why on earth would anyone be fecking worried?" Sheila cursed, scrambling to sit up, "As you can see I'm perfectly alright and just about to get ready for the show."

"You're a wee bit late so you are," Roland laughed, throwing his head back, "It's after midnight."

Sheila staggered to the sewing table to retrieve her spectacles and pushed them on in order to look at the time. It was twenty past twelve, which meant she'd been asleep for hours.

'Oh Mother of Mary," she shrieked, staring at the Irishman, "Have you been messing with my clock?"

Roland couldn't speak for laughter. The best he could manage was to shake his head and pick up the empty wine bottle from by the side of the bed. There wasn't a drop left.

Sheila was mortified and ushered the hunk out through the door in one swift motion. She then set about preparing black coffee and rifling through the drawers for aspirin.

The following morning was Easter Sunday and being a devout Catholic, Sheila Hannigan had taken a stroll to the nearest church of her faith for the morning service. Her head still pounded from the additives in the cheap wine but did little to detract from the eloquent tones of the priest conducting Mass.

Sheila had debated whether to take Confession, after all she was in need of both advice and forgiveness at that very moment in time. Counselling for the Chekov dilemma and penance for her constant drinking, smoking and cursing. Still, there would be other towns with other churches, she reasoned and set off back towards the camp site. Perhaps it was due to the psychic's half-asleep constitution that day or her intense day-dreaming as she trotted back up the road, but Sheila didn't notice the couple behind her until a tiny hand grabbed her elbow.

"Sheila, good morning" Luana cooed, "We walk together, ok?'

Turning around hastily, Sheila saw the Chekov couple holding hands and looking very much in love.

"Goodness, I didn't see you there," she admitted, "Were you in the Church just now?"

Sergei, a lithe dark-haired man with a pale complexion, just nodded and left all the talking to his wife, who chatted happily to the older woman all the way back to the site. The conversation was general, discussing the weather, television news and observations from their walk and, Sheila noted, not once did the Russian male attempt to join in. It was very, very, strange indeed.

The next few hours passed at a fast pace, with the circus family practicing their various talents, performing the afternoon show, taking a brief respite and then repeating it all over again. Sheila was extremely busy again but the afternoon ended on a high with a regular customer turning up with a huge bouquet of flowers for her. Apparently, Fred Thompson and his wife Melanie had been so impressed with 'Psychic Sheila's' last prediction that they were brimming with gratitude, they were also pushing twins in a specially converted pram. It was days like that when Sheila felt her talent come to the fore, and lapped up the attention unashamedly.

By six-thirty Sheila Hannigan had changed into a pale pink dress and grey cardigan, having carefully reapplied her make-up and clipped back her unruly dark curls. A few heads will turn tonight, she told herself as she sashayed out through the door, and why the Hell not.

The first person she bumped into was Sergei Chekov. He was limbering up outside his caravan, stretching his arms behind his head and slowly bending at the knees as he exhaled each new breath. Sheila looked down momentarily at her own shapely figure and vowed to lose a few pounds in the Summer.

"Hello Sergei," she trilled, "That looks rather painful."

The young man shrugged and bent forward, the notches on his spine clearly visible through the pale blue leotard, "Is no problem for me."

Sheila bit the end of her nail, nervously trying to think of something else to say, "Where's Luana?"

"Inside," he replied sullenly, glancing towards the trailer, "She get ready her hair."

Sheila smiled softly to show her understanding, although the Chekovs certainly did have a very strange way of speaking English, she thought.

"I'd better go and get my seat then," she told the Russian, "Don't want to be late for the show."

Sergei Chekov didn't turn around as Sheila moved away, but she did hear him grunt something that might have been 'Goodbye.'

It really was the most puzzling and difficult situation. Luana being bruised and having an affair but attending Church with her husband as though everything were hunky-dory between them. The Irish woman was in a complete quandary whether to subtly intervene or let them carry on as they were.

Watching the acrobats closely as she perched on the edge of her seat, Sheila Hannigan saw nothing but a young couple very much in love. Every time they finished a particular stunt Sergei and Luana smiled at each other in adoration, a genuine heartfelt love, which was the cause of Sheila feeling even more confused. If there had been arguments, tension or hard stares between them, her psychic intuition would certainly have detected something, but as it was there wasn't a single movement, look or word between the couple that could signal a rift. Eventually, she sat back and began to enjoy the rest of the show, even laughing heartily as the clowns splattered each other in custard pies and generally caused chaos.

After the show, the Irishwoman knocked on Danger McDougall's door to see if he needed a hand to water his very precious plants, after all he was technically still in recovery.

"Hiya," the stuntman grinned, opening the door wide, "I haven't seen you all day, have you been busy?"

"Run off my feet," she confirmed, "I must have done fifteen readings this afternoon alone."

"Come on in," the hunk offered, "We can have a night-cap."

"Oh, not for me thanks," Sheila told him, "I'm off alcohol for a few days. I overdid things the other night. In fact, I just came to see if you needed me to water the erm…you know what."

"That would be brilliant," the Merseysider whispered, as though conspiring some dangerous plot, "How about I make us a hot chocolate with marshmallows while you're under there?"

"Go on then, pass me the watering-can."

As they sat drinking on Danger McDougall's bunk, it became obvious to her friend that Sheila was tense.

"Is there something worrying you?" he asked gently, "You can tell me to mind my own business if you want, but I can't help noticing a difference in you tonight love. Not the usual chatty girl I know."

Sheila bit her lip, deciding whether to confide her concerns about the Chekovs or not. She didn't want to portray herself as a gossip-monger but then, on the other hand, she didn't know how long she could keep things in without driving herself crazy. Suddenly everything came tumbling out, Luana's bruised leg, Sergei's abrupt manner, the English voice inside the caravan and Sheila's suspicions of something untoward going on between the Chekov couple. She didn't leave a single detail out.

"Blimey," Mr. McDougall sighed, "No wonder you've got your knickers in a twist."

It was there and then, inside the stuntman's caravan that a decision to confront Luana was made. The friends reasoned that they only had the young woman's interests at heart and the sooner something was said or done the better.

"I've got this," Danger McDougall yelled, suddenly jumping up and opening a cupboard, "It belonged to my great-grandad."

In his hands the young man held a Victorian ear-trumpet, as used by the hard of hearing in days gone by.

"Well, what the feck are we supposed to do with that?" Sheila giggled, taking it in her hands.

"We, well you, stick one end in your ear and the other up against the Chekovs caravan," the man explained, "Then you can hear what's going on and we'll confront Luana about it to-morrow."

Sheila turned the object over, running her fingers along the cold brass moulding, "Now just hold on a minute, you said I can stick it in my ear, why me? Why not you?"

"Aw come on," the stuntman whined, pouting slightly, "It's my leg isn't it? You can move much faster than me if anyone comes out, besides you're the one with psychic intuition."

Sheila Hannigan huffed and stormed out through the entry, hitching her dress up with one hand as she carried the old brass contraption in the other, "Holy Mother Mary," she cursed.

The ground was dry thanks to a warm and sunny few days, and most of the circus family had retired for the night. The odd sound of a television set or radio could faintly be heard as the gipsy made her way along to the Russian's caravan but not a soul moved outside. Danger McDougall sat on the step of his trailer wanting to both offer his support and get a birds-eye view of anything unfolding. Sheila waved him back, embarrassed that he was so brazenly sitting there watching her, a very obvious smirk on his face.

"Go back," she hissed through her teeth, "Somebody will see you."

The stuntman didn't move and shook his head in defiance, "Just get on with it woman."

Sheila crept forward until she was crouched directly under-neath the window of the Chekovs home, her knees cracking as she hunched over. A slight murmur came from inside but it wasn't until she had positioned the ear-trumpet properly that the psychic could hear the conversation inside. What she then heard shocked her beyond belief.

"Pass me the biscuits darling," a male voice clearly said, "Not those, the chocolate fingers."

There was then a rustling and a crunch as if a packet was tossed across the room.

"Do you like my new headband that Sheila made?" a woman asked, her accent was that of a born and bred Cockney from London, "It matches my leotard."

"Don't talk to me about her," the man quaffed, his accent having the same lilt as the woman's, "She tried to have a conversation with me this afternoon."

Sheila's eyes widened as she tried to work out who the speakers were. Danger McDougall was waving, trying to get her attention which didn't help, but he was desperate to know what was going on. Sheila moved along towards the voices, hoping to get more clues.

"Well why didn't you talk to her?" the woman was asking.

"Because you know I'm no bloody good at doing a Russian accent Lulu," her partner confessed, "I wish we'd never pretended now."

"Well, there's no going back," the girl warned, "Simon and Louise Baker doesn't have quite the same ring to it as Sergei and Luana Chekov does it now?"

As the penny dropped, Sheila stifled a laugh. Now it all made sense, she thought, no wonder 'Sergei' was reluctant to speak when he was really a London lad with not an ounce of Russian blood in him. She rubbed the bottom of her spine before preparing to stand up but the couple began talking again.

"By the way," 'Simon' was saying, "How's that bruise coming along?"

"Not too bad," his wife told him, "I'm so bloody clumsy falling off the bed like that."

The pair laughed loudly and followed it with kissing.

Sheila pulled the listening device away from ear and hurtled across the field to Danger McDougall.

"Well?" he pressed, "What's going on?"

It took a good fifteen minutes for Sheila Hannigan to stop giggling and wipe the tears from her face, while her friend stood bemused and shaking his head.

"Oh Lord," she cried, "Have I got news for you."

Chapter Four

Simone

Simone Martin was effortlessly stylish. Even when out sitting on the grass in her denim jeans and t-shirt, she looked the pinnacle of chic, casually adding a silk scarf or a pair of kitten heels to her outfit, Simone was the stereo-typical French woman. She was proud of her heritage and spoke with a soft accent, one that had its origins in rural Provence, always maintaining a slight aloofness but still managing to tantalise and seduce those around her.

Sheila Hannigan was, very naturally, in awe of Simone. But it didn't matter how hard she tried to imitate the European woman's style, the result never quite had the same impact as her jeans were a little too tight and her stomach bulged slightly, giving the resemblance of a rounded muffin. There was a certain finesse that the Irish woman lacked, but nevertheless the two had bonded out of being in the minority, the simple fact that they were women in a man's world.

In recent months Simone had turned her hand to baking and often passed by Sheila's caravan to drop off a pan au chocolat or redcurrant tart. Sheila hadn't liked to tell her friend that her taste buds weren't used to such sharp flavours as those found in this particular fruit, but she appreciated the chocolate pastries and devoured them with lust. In return, the gipsy had offered home-cooked meat pies and stews, but they were politely refused, Simone explaining that her palate was more used to fresh fish and salad. Sheila knew that this was true, she only had to admire the French woman's slim figure to see that a healthy and sensible diet prevailed but, for her own dinners, Sheila couldn't help but be drawn to a hearty plate of meat and potatoes as served up in her childhood home.

It wasn't just her style and poise that Sheila marveled at either, you see Simone Martin played a very important role within the circus and it was partly due to her daring feats that that the crowds rolled in night after night. Simone was a knife-thrower. With a brave young assistant tied to a revolving wheel, the French woman would aim her sharpened instruments and always succeed in them penetrating the wooden disk without injury to her accomplice. Then, as if chancing an accidental death were not enough, Simone would be blind-folded for the finale and repeat the action using her sixth-sense alone. Nobody seemed to know how she managed to throw with such accuracy and perfect timing, and during the act there was perfect silence, the audience biting their nails and perching precariously on the edge of their seats, waiting. Afterwards there was always a standing ovation, as Simone pulled away the mask and smiled with perfect white teeth, her assistant bowing to the crowd and soaking up the electrifying atmosphere. The act had mesmerised Sheila Hannigan too, fueling her deep respect for the friend who seemed so perfect. Although as far as the psychic knew, there was something missing in Simone Martin's life.

Having relocated after Easter, the travelling troupe were now settled in a town near the Welsh border. True to the nature of the countryside around them, they shared a barren field with a flock of sheep, recently sheared and bearing branding marks on their rumps, a sure sign that Spring had arrived and better weather was on the way. On the first day of arrival, the workers were as busy as a hive of bees, setting up tents, connecting power and generally rushing to and fro and a gentle buzz of conversation filled the air all around the site. The sheep stood watching, as sheep are prone to do, with blank expressions on their faces, as their habitat became invaded by props and lights as far as the eye could see, a sure sign that the opening night in this particular setting wasn't too far away.

Having endured a peaceful ride in her caravan, except for a few bumps and clattering crockery, Sheila Hannigan emerged from her home and lit up a cigarette.

"Hadn't you better go and start prattling about with your engine or whatever it is you do?" she called to Danger McDougall, who was still reclining on one of the bunks inside.

"I suppose so," he yawned, stretching lazily, "And it's called mechanics, I'll have you know."

Sheila watched as the stuntman hobbled outside. His leg was still a little unstable since the accident but she knew he would carry on regardless.

"See you later," he called, setting off towards his trailer which had been towed in by another truck, "Don't get up to anything while I'm away."

Sheila opened her mouth to throw a cheeky comment back but her friend was already half way across the grass and out of earshot. She watched him wince as he tried to walk normally and thought about the cannabis plants secretly growing out of sight. It didn't matter to her that he smoked the stuff, but she worried that he might suffer long-term effects. Her thoughts rapidly drifted away as Sheila noticed Simone Martin emerging from her caravan a short distance away. Danger McDougall immediately changed his gait, walking upright and puffing out his chest, the limp becoming almost unnoticeable.

A pang of something unfamiliar hit the gipsy quite hard, it wasn't something she recognised but could, quite possibly, have been jealousy. Of course, the stuntman was free to flirt with whomever he wanted to, Sheila reminded herself, they were only friends after all, but it was the way in which Danger Mc-Dougall seemed so eager to impress the French woman that hit home so hard. Not once, in the past few months, had the stunt-man looked at her in the same way as he looked at Simone, that in itself was soul-destroying.

Later, after ironing her frilly blouse and patterned skirt ready for the change of persona into 'Psychic Sheila', the Irish woman picked up her sewing basket and peered inside. Not a single item sat there waiting for repair, a very good sign that Sheila had been busy that week, but it also meant that she had very little to fill her time before customers arrived. There was only so much cleaning and polishing to be done in a small caravan, therefore Sheila decided to cook. Pulling down a recipe book from the shelf, she flicked through until a photograph of a cottage pie caught her eye.

"Ooh yes," she smiled, "Something filling that I can share with McDougall tonight."

It didn't take long to put the meal together, and after fluffing up the mashed potato on top, Sheila slipped the dish into the fridge, ready to cook later.

"Psychic Sheila' received a variety of clients that afternoon, a few pensioners asking more for advice than predictions, two young girls about seventeen wearing shiny purple tracksuits wanting to know if a career in singing would be fruitful and several housewives, bored with their mundane lives and praying for an insight into a future with much more to offer. Sheila was as honest as she dared to be, holding back on a couple of points that she felt might either upset or offend, and everyone went away satisfied that life would be brighter next year.

After changing into her everyday clothes, being careful to apply a little extra lipstick as she stared at her round, middle-aged face in the mirror, Sheila set off towards the arena where Danger McDougall ought to have been perfecting his stunts for the evening performance. He was there alright, in jeans and a leather jacket, strutting backwards and forwards as he calculated the distance needed to leap through a ring of fire which was balanced precariously on top of an old Mini Cooper. A look of deep concentration was on the daredevil's face and Sheila stood back amongst the onlookers, neither wanting to distract her friend or cause unnecessary gossip amongst the other circus men.

"Bon jour Sheila," a silky voice whispered in her ear, "Isn't he magnificent?"

Sheila Hannigan turned slightly, catching a potent whiff of Simone's perfume as she did so, "Yes, he certainly knows how to pull a crowd does Danger McDougall."

The French woman had her lips pursed, as though amused but unwilling to share the joke, "I think you are very fond of him, no?"

Sheila stiffened slightly and turned to face the exotic creature at her side, "We're just friends, that's all."

Simone was pouting, her dark eyes twinkling as she continued to watch the stuntman go through his checklist of safety precautions, "I know, mon amie, I know."

And then she was gone, just as silently and stealthily as she had arrived, leaving Sheila standing alone.

The show was a tremendous success that evening, with a huge crowd and standing ovations for many of the acts and the atmosphere hot with excitement.

Sheila Hannigan watched from her usual spot, being joined half-way through by Danger McDougall, who had finished his outdoor performance some time earlier. Coincidentally, the stuntman arrived just as Simone Martin entered the ring.

"She's a real looker isn't she?" he gushed, unable to take his eyes off the sexy French woman.

"Yes, I suppose she is," Sheila sighed, feeling put out that her friend hadn't noticed the extra effort she'd gone to tonight, with dangly earrings and carefully applied rouge.

They watched the rest of the show in silence, neither having anything to say to the other and all focus directed towards the incredible acts in the circus ring.

As the audience filtered out some time later, Sheila stood up and smoothed down her skirt. Danger McDougall was day-dreaming and didn't notice her move.

"I've made a cottage pie," she announced, "If you'd like to join me for supper."

The stuntman turned his gaze slowly upwards and blinked, "Aw, thanks, you're a real star, but I've got other plans tonight, Simone's invited me to join her, maybe tomorrow eh?"

"No problem," Sheila huffed, a hot flush threatening to creep upwards and turn her face red, "Let me get through, I've got things to do."

Danger McDougall moved his long legs to let the gipsy leave, oblivious to the fact that her feelings had been hurt and her sixth sense was on full alert. It was as he moved that the Merseysider noticed his friend's appearance properly and grabbed her hand.

"You look lovely tonight," he said, but Sheila was already tug-ging her hand away and heading towards the exit, her mind rac-ing and a hint of annoyance settling on her heart.

Sheila Hannigan's evening was saved by Roland O'Hare.

As she stood debating whether to cook the cottage pie or throw it into the dustbin, Roland knocked on Sheila's door, a wide smile fixed on his face.

"Well, if it isn't herself. Are you actually alone tonight dar-ling?" he inquired in his soft Irish accent.

"Oh Roland, what are you doing here?"

"Coming to help you eat that fantastic looking pie," he winked, stepping inside Sheila's caravan and eyeing the oven-proof dish.

"Have you not got anything better to do with yourself Roland O'Hare?" Sheila chuckled, her mood instantly lifting as she switched on the little electric oven.

Roland pulled a bottle of wine from the inside pocket of his leather jacket and sat down at the table.

"How did you know I didn't have company?" she asked dubiously, finding wine glasses.

"Because lover boy's having it away with sexy Simone," the ringmaster blurted out, none too subtly.

"We are just friends!" Sheila retorted indignantly, "He can do whatever he likes!"

"Whatever you say darling," Roland smiled, rolling the last word off his tongue quite seductively.

"Will you be wanting peas with your pie," Sheila asked, in an attempt to change the subject.

Roland O'Hare nodded and grabbed a corkscrew to open the wine, "Oh yes, peas are fantastic."

Later, having enjoyed an amicable supper and then shared jokes over a few glasses of wine, Roland got up to leave, thanking his host profusely for her wonderful hospitality. Sheila waved him on his way.

Then she stopped to look over at Simone's beautiful pink trailer, where the silhouette of two heads could be seen kissing in the window.

The following day, her emotions confused, Sheila stayed in bed much longer than usual, sipping coffee and smoking a number of cigarettes. She hadn't felt this way in a long time.

The peace was disturbed by a loud rapping at the door.

Sheila flung back the sheets and stood glaring at her reflection in the mirror. Her unruly thick curls were tangled like a hastily constructed bird's nest and her blue flannel nightdress was badly creased from all the tossing and turning she'd done in her sleep. Regardless, she shuffled towards the door.

Outside, Danger McDougall stood dressed in his white jumpsuit with his hands on his hips waiting.

"You look like fecking Elvis Presley stood there like that," Sheila cursed, "What do you want?"

"I need the zip fixing," the stuntman stated shyly, pointing down to his nether region, "It won't go up."

"Well go and take the fecking thing off and come back when I've had time to wake up," she grumbled.

"Is everything alright?" the muscly man queried, "You don't seem yourself this morning."

"I'm fine," the Irish woman snapped back, "Just hunky fecking dory."

As she sat simultaneously watching an episode of 'Murder She Wrote' and repairing the stuntman's jumpsuit, Sheila Hannigan tried to snap herself out of her black mood. It wasn't her friend's fault that he'd fallen for someone younger and more beautiful than herself, she reasoned, it had just come at a time when she had thought their friendship might ease her loneliness. Tears suddenly mingled with the cotton thread that lay in the gipsy's lap, causing it to become wet and unusable. She cast the outfit aside and went to the window. Everything was carrying on as normal outside, nobody was arguing, there were no moments of frustration and the sheep just carried on watching.

"Pull yourself together Sheila Hannigan," the woman told herself, "You have the gift, you can do anything you want."

Inside, Sheila was unconvinced that things would be alright, she already knew that there were things developing that were way beyond her control and to intervene would bring dire consequences. The only way forward was to carry on as if everything were alright, and to pray that someday she would get the one untouchable dream that she wished for. Until then she would soldier on in silence.

For Sheila Hannigan the weekend flew past in a flurry of customers, performances, housework and excessive amounts of ice-cream. She slept fitfully and supped on bottles of Thunderbird wine, but having come out the other side of her temporary depression, the gipsy was now ready to take on the world and the first stop on her list was Simone Martin's caravan.

On Monday morning Sheila was up bright and early baking bread and spring-cleaning. She had the little transistor radio on and sang along to her favourite tunes, the top of her list being Russ Abbot's 'Atmosphere', as the words always put in her in a good mood, no matter which side of the bed she'd fallen out of.

As the bread sat rising in a large ceramic bowl, Sheila spruced herself up and took a short stroll into town to treat herself to something new. There weren't a vast array of shops in the Welsh market town but it didn't take long before a suitable purchase was made and she was on her way back to the caravan. Once inside, Sheila closed the curtains and tried on her outfit, pink velour lounge pants and a matching hooded top. It certainly made a change from the floaty dresses and bohemian style skirts that she usually wore, and if truth be told, Sheila was totally out of her comfort zone.

"I need to sit on a bacon slicer for half an hour," she muttered, turning this way and that to gage how big her bottom looked in front of the full-length mirror, "Now where's that girdle I bought last winter…?"

An hour later, with the bread baked and a few bright accessories completing her new look, Sheila knocked on Simone Martin's door. It was answered after a slight delay, during which period the noise of a cupboard door slamming shut could be heard.

"Bonjour Sheila," a rather flustered Simone peered out.

'Hello love," she smiled, "I've made some country loaves and thought you might like one."

"How sweet," the French woman gushed, "Please come in, I'm trying out a new brand of coffee."

"Perfect," Sheila nodded, heaving herself up into the caravan, "I'm parched."

The inside of Simone's home was just as chic and elegant as its owner, the décor being a subtle blend of pink and purple hues, with a variety of ornate frames holding vintage French circus posters. On the bunks sat an array of silk cushions, each one different to the next but all bearing the beaded exotic trademark of faraway lands and romantic escapism.

"Please, take a seat," Simone gestured, "Would you like vanilla in your coffee?"

"Why not," Sheila shrugged, "I'm feeling daring today."

"Qui?" her friend asked, looking mystified.

"Oh, don't mind me," Sheila continued, "Vanilla would be lovely."

A few minutes later, with tiny coffee cups and saucers in front of them, the two women sat amicably chatting about the weather until, rather unexpectedly, Simone changed the subject.

"Sheila, I want to say sorry to you," she began, her long lashes fluttering up and down, "If you are upset about my relationship with Monsieur McDougall."

"Upset? Me?" Sheila joked, setting down her coffee, "Why would I be? I'm delighted for you both."

"Really?" Simone asked, trying to look for changes in her friend's demeanor, "Oh, thank you! You don't know how happy that makes me feel."

The Irish woman stared back, praying that the slight twitch in her left eye wouldn't give the game away, "Of course, it's lovely that you've found each other. I hope it all works out for you."

"Oh Sheila," Simone squealed, "It's been such a long time since Pierre died that I thought I'd never find love again."

Sheila leaned forward, a slight lump in her throat, "Who's Pierre?"

And so, as women have a tendency to do, over the course of the next hour, they indulged in a confidentiality that brought them closer together.

As it turned out, Simone had married Pierre 'Le Magnifique' Martin at the tender age of eighteen, just a few months after having met him at an audition to become the knife-thrower's apprentice. Despite the thirty year age gap, the pair had been devoted to each other until two years earlier when Pierre had suffered a fatal heart attack. Simone explained that she wanted to put some distance, both proverbially and literally, between herself and her beloved France as the memories were just too painful. It was therefore quite soon after her husband's death that she had joined O'Hare's Circus, putting to good use the skills that Pierre had taught her and building a new life for herself overseas.

"And so you see," Simone explained, wiping a tear that threatened to ruin her mascara, "After losing my Pierre with his magical hands, I was very sad. Maybe now I am ready for love once again. Only time will tell."

Sheila patted the other woman's hand and rose, "I'm only over there if you need me love. Take care."

It wasn't until a couple of nights later, just as she was turning around the 'CLOSED' sign for the evening, that Sheila saw Simone again. Looking every inch the glamour puss, the Frenchwoman was smartly dressed in a tight red trouser suit and black leather boots.

"Sheila," she called out, "Are you free after the show?"

"Well now, let me see," the gipsy chuckled, "Apart from my three lovers taking turns to come round, I might have an hour or so left, why?"

Simone looked blankly at her friend, not understanding the joke, "Please come to dinner with us."

"Us?" Sheila repeated, "You and McDougall?"

The knife-thrower nodded, "Of course, I am making something traditional."

Sheila paused for a second, wondering whether she would feel like a gooseberry with the lovers cooing over each other, but Simone was very persuasive and wouldn't take 'No' for an answer.

"No excuses," the woman grinned, "See you later Psychic Sheila."

Throughout that evening's show, Sheila kept thinking back to the afternoon in Simone's caravan when the tale of Pierre Martin had been laid bare in front of her. It wasn't that she doubted anything that Simone has said, but rather more how the afternoon had ended. Still, confidentiality was a part of her profession and it wasn't for Sheila to share the secrets of others. Of course, there was still the little niggle of jealousy in the back of her mind but, if she were realistic with herself, Sheila could see completely how a man would choose the gorgeous Simone over herself. She just hoped that her daredevil friend was ready for a few surprises along the way, which were inevitable in any new relationship.

As time went on, she made a decision. If at any time during dinner the couple hinted that they would rather be alone, Sheila would take her leave, as long as it was after dessert, of course.

Simone Martin had prepared a good deal of the dinner in advance, and by the time Sheila approached the pink caravan, clutching a bottle of French white wine, some strange aromas were already permeating out through the air vent and into the night. She could definitely detect garlic but little else.

"Welcome," Simone greeted, kissing each of Sheila's rosy cheeks.

"Hiya," Danger McDougall smiled from behind his lover, "Thanks for coming, let me take your shawl."

Sheila offered up the bottle of wine but detected a momentary frown on her host's brow as Simone examined the label. Apparently 'vin de table' wasn't an acceptable dinner gift.

As the first course was served, Sheila and Danger McDougall sat blinking at each other across the table with Simone tucking into her meal, oblivious to any problem.

"Are these snails?" Sheila tentatively asked, picking one up with her fork.

"Of course," Simone quipped, dipping bread into the juice on her plate and then sucking at a shell, "Don't you like it Sheila?"

"Well, I can't say I've ever had them before," she answered, keeping her voice level and polite.

"Oh, we eat them all the time in France," the hostess shrugged.

Both diners nibbled at their starter politely but did their best to avoid actually eating anything, except for the warm crusty bread that sat in a basket in the centre of the table.

The next course was slightly better, although the portion size was rather small and the taste very rich.

"Next we have pig cheeks in red wine," Simone's silky voice was saying, "On the side some butter beans and roasted carrots."

Sheila glanced up at Danger McDougall, who was slicing into his dinner like a skater on thin ice, very, very slowly and carefully. She watched the stuntman wince as he took the first mouthful.

Simone chattered away throughout the meal, oblivious to the ordeal to which she was subjecting her guests, although she was slightly mystified as to why they were eating so slowly.

Conversation turned towards hobbies and before long Sheila was confessing to her love of brass ornaments and knick-knacks. Everyone knew that each available shelf in the gipsy's caravan held a collection of horseshoes and animals which took

Sheila no end of polishing but what her two friends didn't know was that the majority of them had been passed down to her from her maternal grandmother.

"So do all the women in your family have a psychic touch?" Danger McDougall asked as he moved the fleshy meat to one side with his knife.

"Oh yes," Sheila admitted, "All the Hannigan women have the gift, although not all of them use it."

"And where are your family now?" Simone interjected.

"Back in Ireland," the gipsy replied, not daring to look up for fear she might give something away, "I don't get to see them very much nowadays."

"To absent families and circus friends," Danger McDougall cheered, raising his glass in a toast, "And to Simone for cooking us a great dinner."

Sheila pursed her lips together to avoid laughing, this might very well be her first and last French meal, she vowed silently.

Dessert was a chocolate mousse, devoured in less than thirty seconds.

"That was incredible," Sheila gushed, licking her lips, "You'll have to give me the recipe."

"Oh, thank you so much," Simone blushed, "I can give you the snail and pig cheek recipes too."

Danger McDougall winked conspiratorially at his friend, waiting for her diplomatic reply.

"Thank you love, but I'm sure I could never make it as well as you do."

After finishing off their night with a glass of brandy, Sheila said goodnight to her friends and headed home. She had initially waited a few seconds for Danger McDougall to put on his jacket and walk her back to her caravan, but the Merseysider was either too wrapped up in his new love, or unused to being a gentleman to take the hint. Simone's door clattered shut behind her and the sound of French music faded into the distance as Sheila made her way across the field. It wasn't a cold night but the wind was beginning to rustle the tress, and shadows lurked, casting an eerie mood on the circus camp.

Lying in bed, Sheila Hannigan reflected on her day. The relationship between Simone Martin and Danger McDougall wasn't bothering her quite so much now and had, in fact, become a healthy distraction from her own worries. She'd only had one niggle during the course of their meal tonight, and that was her own fault for allowing Simone's question about her family hit where it hurt most. It wasn't that Sheila had any dreadful family secrets to hide, but rather that she was unused to anyone asking. Still, it was over and done with now and there were more pressing things to worry about.

Things like Danger McDougall.

On the morning that Sheila had taken coffee with Simone in her quaint pink caravan, something had happened that she had not divulged to her daredevil friend. He was yet in the throes of a new romance, after all, and might think that the gipsy was making up tales to divert the course of his love.

It was after explaining her marriage to Pierre Martin that the beautiful knife-thrower had shared her secret, and stupidly, daring to call her bluff, Sheila had asked a question. One that she now wished could be retracted, and the memory of what she had witnessed with it.

Simone had detailed, at some length, the magnificent and magical powers that Pierre had possessed, both in his skill throwing knives and in his talent as an artist of French circus posters, the latter being plainly visible on display inside his wife's trailer. Sheila had commented on the art and looked closely at Monsieur Martin's work, which was both vibrant and eye-catching.

However, it was Simone's unwavering belief that Pierre had magical powers with his knives that now caused Sheila some gut-wrenching concern. It was almost as if the French woman believed that her late husband's hands actually held some strange wizardry inside them, and despite Sheila having supernatural powers of her own, she had done the unthinkable. She had laughed.

Sheila Hannigan's cackling had stopped abruptly a few seconds later, turning instead to a dreamlike horror. Simone Martin had opened up a cupboard and removed something wrapped in a piece of black cloth. Carefully removing the outer layer, she had revealed a large glass jar, filled with embalming fluid and containing something precious. Inside were Pierre Martin's hands.

Chapter Five

Reckless Ray

Raymond Stubbs was a huge hulk of a man, standing over six feet tall with muscles of iron, it was even rumoured that he could crack a walnut between his buttocks, but witnesses were few and far between, obviously shy to admit that they'd witnessed such a feat. No matter his immense strength and powerful stature, Raymond was a mild-tempered and well-mannered man, never heard to utter a profanity and always the first to open doors for the ladies and never one to shy away from a favour if ever one were needed. He was somewhere between forty and fifty years old, nobody knew exactly where on that scale, but as with many of the circus performers, age was a seldom talked about topic of conversation. Besides, people were usually too engrossed in watching Raymond lift double his bodyweight than engage in idle chatter about where and when he was born, and the gentleman was content with it that way.

Sheila Hannigan liked Raymond. There was something about the professional strongman that made her feel protected, not just physically but emotionally too, and she particularly liked his sense of showmanship, Ray having cultured a thick handlebar moustache to fulfill his role. He was a natural born joker too, always in the centre of a group telling tales from his youth, or parading around the camp in his leopard-print performance outfit pretending to be Tarzan. On the rare occasion that Mr. Stubbs took to his bed through illness or injury, he would bounce back to full health again with hours, and it was this unnatural resolve that caused everyone who knew him to hold Ray in the highest regard. He earned the nickname 'Reckless', however, from performing some of the craziest acts of strength ever seen.

By the middle of May, the circus had moved down the Welsh coast to a busy sea port, abounding with tourists and tickets to the nightly show were selling fast. The campsite itself was in a field adjoining a caravan park, belonging to the same landowner, and permission had kindly been granted for the travellers to make good use of the facilities nearby which, to the delight of the performers included automatic washing-machines, a plentiful supply of hot water showers and a well-stocked convenience store.

Sheila Hannigan had been the first to load up a washer and then browse the shelves of the shop, treating herself to frozen potato waffles and tins of assorted biscuits. It wasn't that she wasn't trying to eat healthily, but the temptation of such treats was just too much for her will-power and soon her little wire basket was laden with calories in all shapes and forms, even queueing up at the till had caused the gipsy to cast an eye over the array of chocolate bars placed strategically near the exit for such a purpose as over-enthusiastic buyers and one, or maybe two, found their way into her grocery pile.

"Planning a chocolate-fest in front of the telly?" came a loud booming voice across the store.

Sheila looked sheepishly around, dearly hoping that the speaker wasn't addressing her.

"I say, are you planning to eat all that by yourself?" joked Raymond Stubbs, moving into view just as Sheila reached the check-out, "I'm quite partial to a Mars bar."

Sheila flushed and looked down at her goods. She had gone a bit overboard with the treats, but to put anything back now would draw even more attention to herself, so she stood her ground and smiled.

"Morning Ray," she said cheerfully, "It doesn't matter about a few extra pounds at our age does it?"

The strongman sidled up behind her at the counter, emptying his own shopping onto the conveyor belt as he did so, "Of course not, and you look bonnie on it Sheila."

The psychic quickly stuffed her goodies into a carrier bag, paid the cashier and looked down at her friend's items. Ray Stubbs was buying yoghurt, fresh fruit and an assortment of vegetables, putting her own bad habits to shame.

"Hang on and we can walk back together," Raymond offered, "I'll even carry your shopping for you."

Arriving back at her caravan after an amiable conversation on the short walk, Sheila offered Ray a cup of coffee, a natural instinct given that the circus family were so close, and besides, she'd appreciated not having to carry her heavy bag across the field.

"Go on then," the strongman smiled, showing a wide gap in his front teeth, "That would be very nice."

Sheila opened one of her recently purchased packets of biscuits and offered it across, hoping that Raymond wouldn't take the bourbon creams which were her favourite.

"No thanks," he replied, shaking his head, "Coffee's bad enough but I can't ruin my diet by eating biscuits as well. I'll be making myself an omelette shortly anyway."

Sheila was a bit taken aback by the man's strict regime and her facial expression changed to one of shock. "What, you can't even have a couple of biscuits?"

"Well, I could," Ray chuckled, "But it wouldn't do my body much good."

"So what was that about being partial to a Mars bar?" Sheila questioned with a smile on her lips.

"Ah, now those were created to help you work, rest and play" Raymond chuckled, proceeding to sing the jingle from the television advertisement for the chocolate bar.

Sheila shook her head and passed over a steaming cup of coffee, he was such an amicable man.

As they sat passing the time of day, minus the biscuits as Sheila couldn't bear to eat alone, there was a holler from outside and Roland O'Hare appeared with a torn jacket.

"Hey there Ray," he shouted through the caravan door, on seeing that Sheila had company, "Can't stop, I've got to run me Da into town so I have."

"I'll have this ready in an hour or so," Sheila called after the retreating ringmaster as he raced back across the field, "Drive carefully."

When she turned back towards the little table, Raymond Stubbs had picked the morning newspaper and was staring at the front page photograph of Diana Dors, his mouth open and eyes wide.

"Such a sad loss," Sheila commented, picking up her china mug, "She was a great actress."

"What?!" exclaimed Ray, "She's dead?"

"Well I should bloody well hope so," the gipsy cursed, "It's her funeral today. Says so right there."

The weight-lifter squinted at the print, screwing his eyes up tightly.

"Here, try these," Sheila tutted, pushing her reading glasses across to him, "You need to get your eyes tested."

"Maybe," Raymond murmured, still looking devastated from the loss of one of his favourite television personalities, "She was a real smasher."

"She died about two weeks ago," his companion went on, "Didn't you read about it then?"

"I rarely get a daily paper," Mr. Stubbs confessed, "And by the time I've had a wash and some supper at night, I'm usually too tired to watch the late news. I do record the soaps though, I love those."

"Go on," Sheila urged, "Take that paper with you and have a read this afternoon."

"Thanks," the man replied slowly, "Thanks very much."

A couple of nights later, sitting in her usual spot in the back row of the Big Top, Sheila took it upon herself to watch Raymond Stubbs' act very closely, wanting to gage whether his eyesight was affecting his ability to perform. However, she needn't have worried herself unduly as everything went off like clockwork with the strongman not only catching the clowns as they spring-boarded into his arms, but managing to swing them high above his head as the audience cheered. It tickled her immensely too, when an unrehearsed gesture saw a custard pie fly through the air and hit Raymond smack in the face, which caused him to chase the clowns around the ring in mock anger, making the crowd roar even more.

Afterwards, Sheila made her way to the staff entrance and congratulated the trio on their hilarious antics.

"Oh, you nearly made me pee my pants," she confessed to Judy Robinson, the female of the two clowns.

"Ha, ha, made it look like we were having a proper barney didn't they?" interjected Ray Stubbs, appearing through the curtain with a sweaty towel around his neck, "Love this pair to bits."

The clowns, who also happened to be midgets standing less than three feet tall, started pinching the strongman's legs in jest until he chased them out of the tent, leaving Sheila having a fit of giggles.

"They'll be the death of me," Raymond chuckled, returning to Sheila Hannigan's side, "That custard pie was totally unexpected though, really made the night."

"Oh, it certainly did," she agreed, "Funniest thing I've seen for a long time."

"Want to join me for a night-cap?" the huge man suddenly asked, taking Sheila aback.

"Oh, not tonight," she politely refused, "I've promised myself an early night. Goodnight Ray."

The strongman watched her walk to her caravan, wondering what he'd said that had made his friend retreat so quickly, but he wasn't offended. If there was one thing that Raymond Stubbs didn't understand it was women, never had and probably never would.

Meanwhile, Sheila was fighting the laughter. What was it with these men who kept offering her night-caps?

By the weekend, Sheila had caught up on all her laundry, feeling thoroughly spoiled that she'd had the use of an automatic machine all week, instead of having to wash her clothes by hand, and was sitting in the cosy launderette, waiting for the last load to finish inside the tumble drier. As she struggled with the last clue on a crossword puzzle, the door opened, causing a gust a wind to blow her skirt up.

"Feck," she cried, flapping at the flimsy fabric, "Me knickers will be on show to all and sundry."

"No, only to me," Raymond Stubbs teased, closing the door behind him, "And I promise I wasn't looking."

Sheila blushed, "Do you need a hand working the washer?"

"I'm a dab hand at this," Ray told her, "It's been great having this luxury all week hasn't it?"

"Certainly has," she agreed, sticking the biro in her mouth as she pondered the final clue, "Ray, what could this be? I'm damned if I can see the answer."

The strongman glanced briefly at the magazine grid and shook his head, "No idea."

"It'll drive me mad if I don't finish it," Sheila groaned, biting down on the pen, "Somebody must know where the Dalai Lama lives!"

"Oh, that'll be Potala Palace," Ray told her unexpectedly.

"I thought you just looked at it," she frowned, "Yes, it fecking fits as well!"

"Couldn't see the clue properly," Raymond admitted, "Easy answer though."

Sheila threw the magazine down onto the seat next to her and squinted up at her friend, the sun shining in her face and preventing eye to eye contact.

"Haven't you been to get your eyes checked yet?" she demanded, feigning alarm.

"They're alright, honest," the muscular man promised, "Don't fuss."

"Alright, if you say so, I'll have to believe you so I will," she warned, her Irish accent becoming thicker as Sheila fretted, "Men are useless when it comes to taking care of their health.

Raymond Stubbs had crossed to the other side of the room and was carefully measuring washing powder into a plastic cup, his face rigid and tired, but he still listened to the woman muttering under her breath.

That evening after the show, there was much merrymaking. Roland O'Hare senior had arranged for the local farmer to bring over a suckling pig and the beast was hung up between two poles and lifted onto a blazing fire. Danger McDougall had borrowed the circus master's pick-up truck and fetched bottles of cider and bread rolls, making for a succulent feast of roasted pork washed down with alcohol.

As she mingled with crowd, Sheila reflected upon the reasons why she had stayed with the circus. It was times like these, when the invisible bond was tight, that she loved this group of misfits.

None of them belonged in everyday society, and each of them were unique, all with some special talent that had taken them years to hone to perfection. She looked around. Danger McDougall was standing watching the flames rise higher, with his arms tightly around Simone Martin's waist, Luana and Sergei Chekov were sharing a bottle of cider and laughing as they watched Jake Collins balance an apple on his head and there, stoking the fire, was the young and handsome Roland O'Hare, enough to make her heart melt.

"He's a good-looking lad isn't he?" Raymond Stubbs whispered into the psychic's ear.

Sheila Hannigan turned, fighting down the fury that bubbled in her throat, "I hadn't noticed," she lied.

"Come on," Ray laughed, nudging her elbow, "There's a special bond between the two of you, anyone with their wits about them can see that."

"You really do need to go and get your eyes tested," Sheila joked, playing the situation down, "I'm nearly twenty years older than Roland O'Hare so I am."

Ray Stubbs gave a sigh and handed Sheila a cup of cider, "Bottoms up, you crazy woman."

Sheila clinked her cup against his, having to stretch slightly to do so, and smiled to herself. It was true, she did have a special bond with Roland, but luckily not too many people noticed it.

The following morning, with a big clean-up operation in progress, Sheila combed the field with a dustbin liner, picking up litter and ensuring that nothing was left behind. The circus troupe relied on being asked to return to each venue the following year and leaving a trail of rubbish behind them was a sure way to gain a poor reputation. Everyone was out, dressed in their scruffy work clothes, ensuring that nothing went unturned, all except for Roly O'Hare, the gaffer, who leaned against the bonnet of his truck with an AA map spread out in front of him. Sheila sighed, that guide was a sure sign that they would be on the move again the very next day, to pastures new. As long as the sun was shining she didn't care.

"Hey Ray," she suddenly heard Roly shout, "Where's Fisher's Lock? It's in your neck of the woods isn't it?"

Raymond Stubbs appeared from behind one of the big wagons and scratched his head, "Aye, it's about ten miles south of Gorsey Head, shouldn't take us more than an hour and a half."

Roly O'Hare snatched up his atlas and carried it across to where the strongman was sweeping up a pile of wrappers, his large shovel-like hands making light work of the task.

"Show me on the map would you?" the gaffer asked, gesturing to the map, "I'm damned if I can see it."

Ray glanced momentarily at the outline of the coast and shook his head, "Sorry it's no good without a pair of glasses, the print's too small."

"Give it here," Roland the younger called, approaching the two men, "It's like the blind leading the blind."

Sheila stood watching as the handsome man folded the paper to show the designated spot, and then took a pencil from his shirt pocket to show the exact position of the town.

"Right, thanks son," muttered Roly, "At least somebody around here has decent eyesight."

Ray Stubbs slowly returned to his task, a slight flush colouring his cheeks. That's the third incident now, Sheila thought, and as soon as we reach the next campsite I'm taking Ray to the optician.

The gipsy thought no more about the weight-lifter that day, as she was unexpectedly busy in her role as 'Psychic Sheila', dishing out pockets of information, foretelling events yet to happen and soothing the hearts of those who wished to make contact with a relative or friend on the other side. In fact, it wasn't until she turned the 'CLOSED' sign on her caravan door at six o'clock that Sheila really had an opportunity to catch up with any of the performers and, as she sat in her usual spot watching the final show in this delightful seaside resort, it was gone nine-thirty before the Big Top closed its canvas doors and turned out the lights. Slowly making her way back across the field, Sheila waved to Simone Martin who was sitting on the doorstep of her pink trailer taking off her boots.

"It is a lovely evening is it not?" Simone smiled, "A perfect night for romance, no?"

"Chance would be a fine thing!" Sheila exclaimed, giggling at the very thought, "Who in their right mind would have me, eh? He'd have to be blind, deaf and daft!"

As soon as the words had left her lips, Raymond Stubbs appeared around the corner with a spring bouquet of tulips in his arms.

Simone, feeling that her presence was no longer required, blew Sheila an imaginary kiss and went indoors, winking at her friend as she did so.

"Would you like these?" Ray enquired, oblivious to the exchange between the two women.

"What are you doing buying me flowers Raymond Stubbs!" Sheila demanded, putting her hands on her hips, "You'll have the gossip-mongers saying all sorts about me."

"Well, actually I didn't," the strongman confessed, "A lady in the audience sent them backstage for me, as a thank you for pulling her son out of the way of a car yesterday."

"Oh," she replied tersely, "You didn't tell me about that. You're a hero then?"

"Not really," Ray shrugged, "Anyone would have done the same."

Sheila examined the man's face, honest and kind, and decided to cut him some slack, just this once.

"Well, they're lovely," she smiled, taking the flowers, "And they'll brighten up my little home a treat."

"No problem," Ray grinned, "Well, I'd better let you go."

"Come on," Sheila offered, "Let's have a brew before turning in."

It was actually midnight before Sheila Hannigan closed the door behind her guest, having enjoyed a few hours of jovial conversation and several pots of tea. She couldn't help but like Raymond, he had a real charm and innocence about him, besides his great physical stature. She also loved to watch the way in which he twiddled his huge handlebar moustache when he was nervous, making him look like a character from an antiquated Victorian sideshow. They'd talked about all manner of subjects that night, from favourite foods to who was doing what in the long-running soaps on television, which both had a penchant for and never missed recording when they were otherwise oc-cupied. Raymond hadn't given up much about his childhood, and Sheila wasn't one to pry, but she got the general impression that he was from the South-West of the country, and a little more prying soon yielded the information that he was born just a few miles from where they would be setting up camp tomorrow.

The following morning, as her caravan trundled along coun-try lanes, towed by Roland O'Hare's flat-bed truck, Sheila peered out at the changing scenery. All within the space of an hour they had travelled a tranquil coastal road, sped down a busy dual-carriageway and then bumped down winding lanes to reach the southern port that would host the circus for the coming week. The view was breath-taking. White-washed cot-tages sat side by side along the harbour, colourful fishing boats a mere speck on the horizon and the bluest water Sheila had ever seen. Of course, up close it wasn't nearly so shimmering and turquoise but from the steep road down which they were now headed, it looked incredible. Sheila thought that she might even go down and dip her toes in the sea later, if she had time, but for now she was happy to enjoy the ride from the bunk inside her home.

Rap rap.

"There's always someone knocking on that blessed door," Sheila cursed, springing up from her seat, "Who is it?"

Raymond Stubbs gently turned the handle and peered inside, "Sorry to bother you," he said sheepishly, "But as this will be our only free night, I'm going to my mother's for dinner. Care to join me?"

"No, you're alright Ray," Sheila quickly returned, "I wouldn't want to put her to any trouble."

"It's no trouble," he grinned, "She wants you to tell her fortune."

"Oh," she sniffed, taken aback by the comment, "In that case, how can I refuse?"

"Great," Ray Stubbs replied shyly, twirling his enormous moustache between his fingers, "If you're sure you don't mind. We'll leave here at six."

Sheila nodded, signalling her agreement, she didn't mind at all.

"What'll I wear?" she yelled, seeing Ray start to close the door again, "Is it formal?"

The strongman stuck his head back inside Sheila's caravan again, laughing merrily, "There are no airs and graces in our house," he told her, "Wear what makes you feel comfortable."

Sheila said that she would, but spent the rest of the afternoon pulling clothes out of her cupboard, looking for matching accessories and momentarily toying with the idea of going out in her carpet slippers.

True to his word, Raymond Stubbs was ready a six o'clock on the dot and pipped the horn of his truck to let Sheila know he was waiting. She emerged after a few seconds, resplendent in floaty floral dress and strappy sandals, wooden beads and bangles completing the look.

"Is it far?" she asked, carefully placing her crystal ball on the passenger seat and then climbing up behind it with a slight struggle due to her short, chubby legs.

"No, we'll be there in ten minutes," Ray assured her, "We could have walked but the coastal path is a bit stony, didn't want you to ruin your summer shoes."

Sheila let out a sigh of relief. She wasn't averse to the idea of exercise but she was astutely aware that the most movement she'd indulged in all week was lifting a wine glass to her lips, so a stroll across the cliffs would most definitely have seen her out of breath before they'd reached the first stile.

Mrs. Stubbs lived in a fisherman's cottage in the next village, set amidst lush countryside on one side and a thick, dense forest on the other. It looked like a good setting for a horror film, Sheila thought to herself as she watched the crows fly out of the trees and sit on a fence, although the cottage itself looked well cared for and idyllic.

"Oh, my boy," wailed a tall willowy woman, rushing out from the open door, and around to the driver's side of the truck, "Welcome home."

Raymond jumped out and hugged his mother tightly, burying his face in her neck as she held him close. It was several minutes before the pair finally separated and turned to address Sheila.

"Hello love," the woman said serenely, ushering them inside, "So pleased to meet you."

"You too Mrs. Stubbs," Sheila replied politely, "And whatever you're cooking smells delicious."

"Roast chicken," the older lady revealed, and then lowering her voice said, "My Raymond's favourite."

Sheila followed her into a small sitting room, full of overstuffed chairs in various shades of green.

"Push him off there," Mrs. Stubbs instructed, motioning to a scruffy black dog who lay on the arm of the sofa, "And tell me all about yourself dear."

Sheila squirmed uncomfortably, "There's plenty of time for that after you've caught up with Ray," she said.

And so, the evening sped by in a flurry of laughter, reminiscence and over-indulgence on the delicious roast dinner set before them. The threesome sat watching one of their regular soaps too, each in turn commenting on who was doing what and guessing the next storyline. Sheila watched as the mother and son bounced anecdotes off each other as only close relations know how and admired the respectful way in which Raymond had insisted upon washing up the plates while his mother had her fortune told.

Unsurprisingly, Mrs. Stubbs had complete faith in what 'Psychic Sheila' revealed to her and nodded enthusiastically every time a new fact or prediction was revealed. Unfortunately for the gipsy though, it wasn't all plain sailing and visions from Raymond's childhood kept coming to the fore, causing her to stop, focus and regather her thoughts. Eventually the crystal ball misted over once again, signalling that there was no more to tell for this particular customer.

Sheila sat back against the sofa cushions and gratefully accepted the cup of tea that Ray had brought them, looking at him with renewed interest but keeping her lips sealed.

"Do you know, when he was a little boy, we all used to call him Reckless Ray," Mrs. Stubbs chuckled, glancing over at her son, "He was fearless, into everything."

Sheila Hannigan smiled, it was easy to imagine given Raymond Stubbs' current profession.

"Whoever would have thought he'd end up in the circus," the woman continued, her shoulders jigging up and down, "If only his father could see him now."

The psychic reflected upon the close-knit family scene that her crystal ball had conjured up just a short time ago, "I'm sure he would have been very proud," she commented.

"Well, anyway," Mrs. Stubbs concluded, rising to her feet, "You youngsters will be wanting some time to yourselves this evening, so I'll make myself scarce."

"No!" Sheila blurted, "We're not, erm, we're just friends."

The mother looked at her son and then across at the beautiful and mysterious Irish woman sitting before her, "Oh, I'm sorry, It's just that Raymond's never brought a girl home, I thought...."

"Mam" Ray interrupted, his face glowing crimson, "We'd better be getting back anyway."

Mrs. Stubbs nodded, the disappointment of her beloved son's love life, or lack of it, etched upon her face.

"Thank you Sheila," she said slowly, "You truly have the gift of sixth sense."

On the drive back to the campsite, Raymond Stubbs tried to apologise for his mother's forthrightness but Sheila dismissed it as the enthusiastic ruminations of a zealous parent.

"You should have seen the frightful boys my Dadda tried to get me hitched to," she laughed, revealing just a hint of what her life back on the Emerald Isle had been like, "It would make your hair curl."

Ray laughed, a genuine throaty noise, causing tears to prick at the corners of his eyes.

"Anyway," Sheila continued, "On a serious note, we have something urgent to attend to."

The strongman shot her a sideways glance but then turned his focus back to the winding road ahead.

"Oh Sheila," he groaned, remembering the gipsy woman's constant nagging about his failing eyesight, "You're not going to force me to go to the optician's are you?"

Sheila tutted and put her hand on her friends thick forearm, feeling his thick bristling hairs under her fingers, "There's nothing wrong with your eyesight Raymond Stubbs."

Ray stopped the truck abruptly and turned to face her, waiting for an explanation.

"You had no problem watching Coronation Street earlier," she told him, choosing her tone carefully, "Or any other night for that matter, so I know there's nothing wrong with your vision."

The man beside her didn't utter a word but sat stiffly waiting for the punchline.

"But," Sheila told him softly, "You couldn't see the newspaper, nor help me with my crossword, so from that I realised that you can neither read nor write."

Raymond sighed, "I don't know what to say…"

"Say yes," Sheila chuckled, nudging him in the ribs jokingly, "Yes, to letting me teach you."

The huge man turned the key in the ignition, a wide smile spreading across his face, "Yes."

Chapter Six

'Punch' & Judy Robinson

As the days turned to weeks, Sheila Hannigan found herself busier than ever before. In between her psychic readings she was spending hours mending and altering clothes for the crew, baking treats for her friends and, true to her word, teaching Ray Stubbs how to read and write. The huge man was progressing well under Sheila's careful tuition and the pair found comfort in each other's company, although the prying eyes of the rest of the circus folk hoped that a romance was blossoming. However, if you'd asked the gipsy about any rapid beating of the heart, she would have laughed and shrugged it off as nothing more than a close friendship.

The circus had now moved inland to the country's capital city, where throngs of eager customers were snapping up tickets like they were going out of fashion. It was also the height of summer and, given the busy location, was set to be a record-breaking financial success for Roly O'Hare and his performers. It had been decided early on that the troupe would stay in the city for the duration of the school holidays, spanning mid-July to the end of August, and promises of a bonus payment to each worker, whether it be a member of the rigging crew or the Big Top's star attraction, had everyone in high spirits.

Two days into the move to the city site and 'Psychic Sheila' was booked up for the whole week in advance, with both afternoon and evening readings, pushing her to the limit, although she still had her mornings free and had vowed to rise earlier than usual to make the most of the glorious summer sun. On this particular day, she was making flapjacks at seven in the morning, filling her caravan with the wonderful aroma of sticky syrup and warm oats. In the background the Pet Shop Boys sang 'West End Girls' on the little transistor radio, fitting lyrics considering their current location, Sheila mused.

"Well, well," tutted Roland O'Hare junior, sticking his head part way through the open window, "There she is, Delia Smith herself! Something in there smells fantastic, so it does."

Sheila chuckled and threw her damp tea towel at the young man's face, "You can wait until they've cooled down Roland. Trust you to smell my flapjacks from out there!"

"Oh, I think you'd better make more than one batch," Roland joked, "We can smell them right across the field. You'll have a queue as long as my arm in a minute or two."

Sheila watched him disappear and then turned to make more treats, intending to share with everyone.

An hour later, after using up every plastic container and empty biscuit tin that she could find, Sheila Hannigan set off to make deliveries.

This is the new me, she told herself confidently, loving thy neighbour and being a good Samaritan.

First call was to Roly O'Hare, the cantankerous old circus owner, who eyed the gipsy curiously as she offered a tub of freshly baked flapjacks to go with his morning brew.

"What's all this in aid of?" he sniffed, taking off the lid and peering inside, "Have you finally gone mad?"

"Just take it and keep your sarcasm to yourself," Sheila sniffed, "Or if you don't want it…?"

"Now hold on," chirped the gaffer, clutching his treats tightly, "I didn't say that. Thank you Sheila."

She trotted away, on to the next trailer, and the next, until there was only one little tin left and, knocking rapidly on Judy Robinson's door, waited for the three foot female clown to answer.

"Sheila!" the petite woman grinned, "Are those for us? Come on in, please."

"Absolutely," she smiled, handing over the flapjacks, and stepping up into the caravan, "I've made some for everyone. How are you Judy?"

An hour passed as the women chatted over coffee and, realising that she would now be in a rush to get changed for her first onslaught of customers, Sheila made her excuses to leave.

"You know we never get time for a proper catch up," complained Judy, seeing her guest to the door, "We should do this more often love. Have a lovely day."

Stepping down onto the grass, Sheila waved at the dwarfed woman and hurried away, thinking deeply.

It had been a strange experience, going into the home of those two little people, she contemplated, with their silver coffee pot and Art Deco ornaments. They certainly lived in a very comfortable manner, even the bottle of whisky she'd spied on the shelf was single malt of the very best quality. Judy herself had been robed in a silk dressing-gown with an ostrich feather trim, not really the kind of attire that a circus entertainer could afford unless they came from an upper-class background or had won the premium bonds. Walking quickly, her mind racing at the same pace, Sheila mulled everything over for a while, trying to work out whether the Robinson's were in a very special league of their own or if they held a secret.

It was a long tiring day for all the circus performers, and Sheila Hannigan was no exception. In fact, so exhausted was she after the dozen or so readings that day, that the gipsy decided to forego her usual seat in the Big Top, preferring instead to catch up on some television with an early supper. Naturally, she felt a pang of guilt, not being there to support her colleagues, but Sheila felt the urge to listen to her tired and weary body instead, curling up with a mug of hot chocolate and an episode of 'Dallas.'

"Gosh, would you look at those fantastic dresses," she muttered under her breath as one of the characters slid onto the screen, "If I wore that I'd look like a fecking football wrapped in Christmas paper."

Knock, knock.

"Oh Hell," the gipsy cursed, pulling her dressing-gown tightly around her, "Who's there?"

It was Judy Robinson, red-faced and flushed. She'd obviously run across the field at a fast pace.

"Sheila, I need your help urgently," the clown gasped, "I've just split my trouser bottoms and I'm due back in the ring in half an hour!"

"Haven't you got another pair?" Sheila asked with a tinge of impatience in her voice.

"Well, not that will match Paul's costume, and he hasn't got time to get changed."

Paul, was Judy's husband and partner in their comical act as the resident clowns, but the rest of the crew knew him better as 'Punch', as in 'Punch and Judy.'

"Come on then," Sheila sighed, opening the door a touch more, "Get them off quick."

As Sheila worked away on her Singer sewing machine, Judy Robinson sat looking around the caravan and making polite comments about her friend's belongings. It wasn't often that the two women had time to sit and chat, and as time was now of the essence, there was little to be said. Sheila secretly smiled to herself as she watched the dwarf dangling her little legs off the bunk and wondered how many tasks in life would be made so much more difficult by being born a midget but she was too polite to raise the question. And so, within ten minutes, the tiny trousers had been repaired as good as new and Judy pulled them back on, thanking Sheila profusely as she did so. The gipsy shook her head, saying it was no problem at all.

"Except, I didn't get to find out who shot J.R. Ewing!" she mumbled, closing the door with a bang.

The following morning, Roland O'Hare was taking a short drive to the East End of the city, where a huge street market was set up selling all manner of goods from clothing to fruit and vegetables. Being a thoughtful chap, he'd invited Sheila along for the ride.

"Holy Mother Mary," the gipsy croaked, holding her seat tightly as Roland manoeuvred his truck through the busy traffic, "You'll get us killed so you will."

"Ah, lighten up," he laughed in response, "My driving is safer than that underground train thing."

Sheila had to agree, she really didn't fancy being stuck below the earth's surface with hundreds of commuters rushing around beside her and crushing her shopping bags.

Trying to take her mind off the road ahead, she decided to touch on a subject that had been bugging her.

"Roland," Sheila ventured in her soft and soothing Irish accent, "How well do you know the Robinson's?"

"Punch and Judy?" he chuckled, "Well enough, why?"

"Well, I don't want to sound like a gossip or anything," Sheila began, folding her hands in her lap, "But I noticed that they seem to have a lot of expensive stuff in their caravan. I just wondered how they could afford to live the way they do, unless your Da pays them extra…"

"What? My Da pay them more?" the young man spluttered, his eyes still fixed on the cars in front, "You must be joking!

They get paid the same as everyone else, I can assure you of that darling. Look, I'll be honest with you, I haven't ever been inside their home, so I wouldn't know what you were talking about."

Sheila cast her mind back to the expensive ornaments and Judy's rather fetching ostrich feather robe.

"Do you think they could come from a wealthy family?" she suggested as they turned into a side street.

"I don't think so," Roland sighed, parking the truck in the first available space, "They don't come across as being any more educated than you or me. Now, I've some tools to buy and I'll be guessing that you'd rather look at clothes and trinkets, so I'll meet you back here in an hour, is that ok?"

Sheila said that it was and walked off towards the market, still brooding over her height-challenged friends. She wished that she hadn't mentioned it to Roland O'Hare now as he probably thought her jealous of the clown's lifestyle, but it was definitely a mystery waiting to be solved. Besides, Psychic Sheila's natural intuition told her that something was afoot and she needed to get to the bottom of it.

Sheila Hannigan's sole purchase from the busy market was a feather duster. Not any ordinary synthetic duster, but one made up of natural plumes from some kind of soft fluffy chicken or duck, and she was as proud as could be about her bargaining skills too.

"Ha, ha, is that all you've bought?" Roland teased, loading an armful of tools into the back of his truck, "You can tickle me with it anytime darling."

Sheila blushed and climbed up into the passenger's seat, "Don't speak to me like that Roland O'Hare," she scolded, "It's not right. Now come on, I've got some dusting to do."

Back in her caravan, with the windows wide open and the door ajar, Sheila Hannigan put her new purchase to the test by clearing all her ornaments off the shelves and sliding the feather duster along each surface. It was only when she went to put each item back in its regular spot that the woman noticed something odd. There was a china figurine missing and it was the only one that was worth any money.

Sheila looked again at the ornaments she'd put on the table and then all around her. There was very little space in which a porcelain figure could get lost but it definitely wasn't there. She thought carefully, casting her mind back to that morning. The caravan door had definitely been locked, as she'd had to use her key to open it on returning from her trip out with Roland, so nobody could have been inside. Switching on the kettle, Sheila tried to remember the last time she'd definitely seen it and couldn't remember exactly, although she did recall picking it up to clean the previous week.

Frustrated and mithered, Sheila carried on with her day, juggling psychic readings, costume changes and then finally, as the curtain went up, she sat in the Big Top waiting for the show to begin.

"Alright Sheila?" Roly O'Hare queried, slipping into the seat beside her, "Roland mentioned that you thought Punch and Judy were living beyond their means…"

Sheila cursed under her breath, composing herself before replying, "He had no right to say anything Roly. Besides, it's probably just me overreacting."

"I wouldn't be so quick to dismiss it," the older man told her, discreetly popping a square of chewing tobacco into his mouth, "I've noticed a few strange things myself, like empty champagne bottles and takeaway cartons in the bin every night of the week."

Sheila pursed her lips, thinking, "Champagne? Goodness me, that's some lifestyle."

"What do you reckon we do a bit of spying?" Roly suggested, still not taking his eyes off the performers in the ring, "You could use your psychic powers?"

"My powers are not to be abused," Sheila told him sharply, "I'm sure we can get to the bottom of it by natural means. Besides, it's hard to get up to anything untoward around here without somebody finding out!"

"Aye it is," Roly conceded, looking her up and down, "Like sneaky trips to the market."

Sheila puffed out her cheeks trying to control the anger which had brewed up inside but, before she could think of a cutting remark with which to reply, the circus owner had gone, leaving the woman staring at his retreating figure as he ducked under the canvas sidings.

"Damn you Roly O'Hare," she breathed, flaring her nostrils and glowering, "I hate your guts."

Several people in the row immediately in front of Sheila turned around, annoyed that she had cursed in front of their children but she wasn't fazed. Nothing would appease her tonight.

It wasn't until a couple of days later that Sheila was called upon by Judy Robinson, once again in need of a favour and, just like the previous time, she was in a hurry.

"We've bought these new outfits," the clown explained, "But obviously they'll need altering to fit our, erm, short stature."

Sheila held up the shiny material and sighed, "Well I can certainly sew them to fit, obviously Punch will have to pop over to be measured too, but it'll take me the best part of tomorrow morning."

Judy Robinson clapped her hands together and then held out her arms to be measured, "I can't thank you enough Sheila. Would you join us later for a fish and chip supper? We'll pay."

The psychic thought for a moment, unsure if she really wanted to be in a situation where she would most certainly put her foot in her mouth by using words like small, little and tiny, which might be taken in the wrong context, but then realised it would be a good opportunity to see the Robinson's caravan again.

"That would be lovely," she agreed, putting down her tape measure, "I'll bring a bottle of wine."

"No need, "Judy smiled, "We've got a fridge full, and it's the best you can buy."

That evening, inside the clown's caravan, Paul Robinson stood on a wooden step in order to pour boiling water into the teapot and chatted merrily to their guest as he did so.

"Have you ever tried Chinese tea Sheila?" he ventured, putting cups on to a tray, "It's green you know, and supposed to be very healthy."

"I can't say I have Punch," Sheila admitted, hoping dearly that it was a regular English tea in the pot, "I'm happy with standard black tea."

"That's what we've got here," the short man assured her, "Proper Yorkshire tea to go with our supper."

"Here we are," Judy suddenly announced, entering the home with a carrier bag full of fish and chips, "Hope I didn't take too long. Oh, Sheila, you're here already."

"Just a couple of minutes," the gipsy replied, "Do you need a hand?"

Judy brushed her away cheerfully and began plating up the meals while Sheila took in her surroundings.

Suddenly she let out a short gasp of breath, stunned at what she had seen.

"Is everything alright?" Punch asked, rushing to Sheila's side, "You've gone as white as a ghost."

The psychic nodded and desperately tried to compose herself, while all the time looking at a porcelain ballerina sitting primly on the Robinson's shelf.

"Yes, I'm fine," she gulped, trying to see if the figurine had a tiny chip on its side like her missing ornament used to. This one had a defect too, in exactly the same place.

"Maybe this will perk you up a bit," Judy announced, waddling over with a plate of food, "Salt and vinegar on the table, help yourself Sheila."

The trio ate their meal, interspersed with idle gossip about the latest goings-on around the camp, until Sheila could hold her tongue no more and prepared herself to ask a direct question.

"That's a grand ornament you have there," she told Judy, nodding towards the delicate dancer, "Do you mind me asking where you got it?"

The frosty glare that was momentarily exchanged between husband and wife in that split second was enough to confirm Sheila Hannigan's fears. The figurine was hers and Judy must have stolen it.

"I don't rightly remember now," the other woman lied, "It must have been a gift some years ago."

Sheila chewed silently on a chip and let her psychic instincts go to work. She had a feeling that this wasn't the only stolen object in the Robinson's caravan.

Up bright and early the next morning, dressed in a maxi skirt and loose top, Sheila Hannigan began her investigation. Armed with a notepad and pencil, she visited each of her friends in turn, asking casually if they had lost anything recently, all under the pretence that she intended to set up a 'Lost Property' bin.

The results were astounding. Danger McDougall's watch had gone missing about a week ago but, despite hunting high and low, he couldn't find it anywhere. It was a family heirloom, he explained to Sheila with a sincere sadness in his voice, brought back from Singapore by his great uncle Henry.

Simone Martin had mislaid a particularly expensive silk scarf, bought some years ago at a chic Parisian department store while Jake Collins couldn't find his antique compass, something that he'd previously used every time they set up camp in order to rig the Big Top up facing southwards.

The Chekovs were missing a transistor radio and even Roly O'Hare confessed to Sheila that he couldn't find a gold pen that he was very fond of. It was time to start digging for clues.

Having logged all the details and returned to her caravan, Sheila sat with a steaming mug of coffee and thought carefully about her options. She didn't trust Roland to keep her suspicions to himself, not after he'd told his father about Sheila questioning him over the Robinson's income but neither did she want to confide in Roly as her loathing for him was increasing as the days passed. The only person whom she felt was totally trustworthy in keeping secrets was Raymond Stubbs but given the close proximity to which he interacted with the clowns every day, she wasn't convinced that he was the right confidante either.

An hour passed, and Sheila's coffee turned cold. A ticking clock was the only noise inside her caravan as she pressed herself to make a plan. If only she could get inside the Robinson's caravan while they were performing in the ring, she could do a quick search for the missing items and then report her findings to the gaffer. But, what if she were caught? What if the clowns returned unexpectedly and accused her of breaking and entering? Sheila wasn't prepared to take that risk and settled upon doing something that she had never done before, something that made her feel utterly and totally ashamed. Blackmail.

Sheila Hannigan and Danger McDougall were the only members of O'Hare's Circus troupe that knew the Chekovs weren't actually from Eastern Europe. She hadn't confided in any of her other friends and felt certain that the stuntman hadn't either, although there was a slight chance that he might confess to Simone one night amidst their pillow talk. However, given her desperation to get to the bottom of the Robinson's apparent wealth and possible kleptomania, Sheila waited until the acrobats returned to their home after the show and carefully laid out her plan.

"I not understand Sheila," Luana Chekov faltered in her strange accent, "We Russian."

"That's just it love," Sheila cooed, brushing her hand upon the young woman's cheek, "I know that you're not, and I know that you're both English. I'm psychic, remember?"

The couple looked at each other and then back at Sheila. Sergei's mouth opened in shock.

"It's alright though," Sheila continued, smiling sincerely, "I won't tell anyone, but I really need your help with something. Do you mind if I pull up a chair?"

The Chekovs didn't really have a choice. They were also slightly terrified at the thought of 'Psychic Sheila's' powers being so insightful that other confidentialities might be uncovered and reluctantly agreed to assist in her quest to find the missing trinkets. Therefore, that night, as soon as their own performance had ended, Sergei and Luana ran from the circus tent to meet Sheila outside.

"Here's the list of what you're looking for," she whispered, handing Luana a piece of paper, "I know they keep their key under the step and don't worry I'll whistle loudly if anyone comes."

"I still don't like this," Sergei moaned, his fake Russian accent disappearing completely now that he knew Sheila had uncovered their secret.

"Shut up," Luana retorted, pinching his arm, "Let's just get this over and done with."

Ten minutes later, pretending to look for four-leaf clovers in the grass, Sheila nodded quickly to Sergei Chekov as he opened the Robinson's caravan door after having finished the search. He was empty handed.

"The stuff on the list isn't there," he told the gipsy, who was instantly disappointed, "But we did find a handful of pawn shop tickets in a drawer."

Sheila brightened and held out her hand, "Let me see."

Each ticket came from the same shop in the city, less than a mile down the road from their current location, and each had an item scribbled upon it. The psychic pushed her spectacles up the bridge of her nose and read each one in turn.

"Gold watch, Hermes scarf, transistor radio, gold pen, antique brass compass. They're all there," she sighed, silently plotting what to do next, "We have to get them back."

"We!" exclaimed Sergei, "Oh no! Leave me and Luana out of this, we've done our part of the bargain."

"Don't worry," Sheila smirked, showing a gold tooth, "I have a plan."

The following morning, straight after breakfast, Sheila arrived unannounced on the Robinson's doorstep. She had the pawn tickets tucked safely in a side pocket and carried her precious crystal ball in her arms.

'Good Morning," she enthused as Punch opened the door, "I've been thinking how to repay you both for the lovely supper the other night."

"Oh, there's no need," the little man replied, "You've done so much for us lately Sheila."

"Nonsense," she continued regardless, "I've come to give you both a free reading, it's the very least I can do. Is now a convenient time?"

"Well, I er…" Punch began, scratching his head and turning to look at Judy who was shuffling off her chair.

"Yes, come in," his wife cried excitedly, "I've always wanted to have my fortune told."

"Grand," Sheila grinned, stepping inside, "Put the kettle on."

"Are you going to read the tea leaves?" Punch asked, slowly stepping up to rinse out the teapot.

"No," the psychic chuckled, carefully taking the cloth from around her crystal ball, "I'm going to see if the mist can clear in this. The tea's because I'm parched."

Settled at the table with Punch and Judy Robinson seated opposite, 'Psychic Sheila' closed her eyes and pretended to go into a trance. She waited a few seconds, before opening them again and then peered into the swirling clouds in her crystal ball.

"Oh Punch," she tutted, "I feel you're carrying a very heavy burden, a secret perhaps."

She sensed the short man nudging his wife and then continued her spiel, "And Judy, there are things that you have done that will bring you great sorrow in the future. I can see stolen things, shiny objects that don't belong to you."

There was tension across the table as the Robinson's faces grew pale.

"The mists are showing me something," Sheila crooned, placing her hands around the glass globe, "They want me to open a drawer, now which one could it be?"

"It must be wrong!" Judy shrieked, "How does it tell you these things?"

"Shhh," the gipsy whispered in hushed tones, "I need to follow what the mists are telling me."

Suddenly, still feigning a trance, Sheila stood up and walked over to the kitchen drawer. She opened it slowly, pretending to listen to some faraway voice for advice, and then pulled the thing open with a jolt. As she did so, keeping her back to the clowns, the psychic deftly put her hand into her pocket and snatched up the pawn tickets.

"What have we here?" she asked, holding the pieces of paper aloft, "I sense that these belong to other members of our community, they do not belong to you."

Judy Robinson burst into tears, covering her face with her tiny hands and sobbed until Sheila sat back down again. Punch got up to pour himself a tumbler of whisky, despite the early hour.

"Now, now," soothed Sheila, "We can sort all this out. Why don't I make us some more tea while Punch goes off to fetch the things from the pawn shop eh?"

"Now, just a minute…" the stunted man began, "It'll cost me a fair amount of money to get all that stuff back, we'll be out of pocket."

"Better than out of a job and sitting in jail though," Sheila commented, avoiding his glare, "You've got an hour to get there and back or I'm going over to fetch Roly O'Hare."

By ten o'clock, Punch Robinson had returned to his caravan and was unloading the contents of a canvas sack onto the table, cursing profusely as he did so.

"Thieving bugger," he mumbled, "That shop owner charged me a fortune. I've lost nearly seventy pounds!"

"Well, you'll just have to eat beans on toast and drink Black Tower instead of champagne won't you?" Sheila scolded, watching closely as the items were set out in front of her, "And don't be too keen to use your sticky fingers again, this crystal ball of mine reveals everything."

"We can't just hand the things back can we?" Judy whined, "I mean, everyone will know that we took it."

"You'll return it all one way or another," Sheila told them, "I don't care how, but you will."

With a final parting shot, she gathered up her magical ball and snatched the porcelain ballerina from the shelf, leaving the midgets to ponder their fate.

A couple of days later, sitting in her usual spot watching the show, Sheila was joined by the all too familiar circus owner, wrapped in a thick duffle coat to keep out the chilly night breeze.

"You were wrong about Punch and Judy," Roly told her, fumbling inside his pocket, "They must have been using up some savings to buy that champagne, I noticed their bin's full of empty tinned tuna cans and cheap plonk this morning."

Sheila didn't say anything for a while but just sat biting her lip. When she did speak it was sincere.

"I guess I got it all wrong then didn't I? Sorry I caused any concern."

"Aye, well," Roly O'Hare sniffed, rolling a thumbnail of tobacco between his fingers, "No harm done."

He rose to leave, but thought of something and suddenly turned back.

"Oh, and Sheila, the strangest thing happened this morning. That gold pen that I thought I'd lost, I found it in my window box, right beside the pansies."

Chapter Seven

Indira Rajpal

As you can imagine, it wasn't easy for the circus folk to attend doctor's surgeries when they had a medical complaint, what with all the moving around and tracking of records. Therefore, to ensure a clean bill of health for all his employees, Roly O'Hare arranged an annual visit from a general practitioner before they left the city limits each summer. For the past three summers, the doctor had been a no-nonsense Indian woman named Indira Rajpal, whose practice was located in one of the capital's poorer areas. She both appreciated the sum of cash and free family tickets to the show that the gaffer passed to her when the check-ups were completed and enjoyed the week or so away from her regular patients. There were rarely any serious ailments amongst the troupe and the visits always left the usually serious doctor with a wide grin on her face. This summer was no different to the previous two, just a slight increase in the age of the patients and the best weather the country had seen for some years.

Sheila Hannigan hadn't slept properly for over a week. After the scenario with Punch and Judy Robinson she was feeling down, having faked her talents to expose them, the psychic now felt at an all-time low. She tried hard to be her cheerful, jolly self but Sheila was so lethargic that even seeing to the demands of her customers left her drained. Caffeine hadn't helped to perk her up either, and by the end of each day the poor woman found herself curled up in a blanket watching hour after hour of television. She didn't really care what Del Boy was up to in 'Only Fools and Horses', nor had she giggled at the antics on the Benny Hill Show, and if truth be told Sheila wouldn't have been able to recount the storyline afterwards anyway, so far away were her thoughts at that time.

On the morning that Doctor Rajpal came calling Sheila was sitting on the doorstep smoking her third cigarette of the day, watching the curling puffs of smoke wind upwards as she exhaled slowly through her nose. Indira Rajpal shook her head and pointed a warning finger.

"I thought we agreed you were going to try to give up that nasty habit," the G.P. scolded, setting her large leather bag down on the grass.

"I tried," Sheila lied, stubbing out the offending item in a china ashtray, "But it didn't work."

The doctor let a smile cross her face before speaking again, she had a great fondness for the gipsy, "Why don't we discuss some quitting methods over a pot of tea? I'm sure I can help."

Leading the way inside, Sheila inwardly wished that she'd locked the door and stayed in bed.

Sitting across from each other at the freshly scrubbed table, the two women eyed each other over their teacups, one sitting stiffly in her professional capacity, the other leaning forward wearily as she fought the urge to tell the doctor that she wasn't up to having a lecture today.

"You look very tired Sheila, are you getting enough sleep?"

"Ha," the psychic snorted, spilling some tea into the saucer, "I'm absolutely shattered if truth be told. I don't suppose there's any chance of you giving me some sleeping pills is there?"

"Sheila," Indira Rajpal began, "You know how reluctant I am to prescribe them, we've been through this in the past. Do you know why you're not sleeping? Is something worrying you?"

The other woman bit her fingernail, reluctant to say too much, "I'm not worried, well, maybe just a bit."

"The old issues?" Doctor Rajpal asked kindly, putting a hand on Sheila's arm, "You need to confront your inner demons my dear, it's no good stewing over things that can't be changed."

Sheila looked up, focussing on a piece of stray hair that had escaped the confines of the doctor's tightly woven bun, "You know I can't let it go, not with things the way they are. I've spent over a decade running away, I really don't know how much longer I can run, I'm out of steam, so I am."

"Let me examine you properly," Indira soothed, pulling a stethoscope and arm cuff with a pump from her bag, "I need to check your blood pressure and your heart."

Sheila unbuttoned her blouse and allowed the doctor to examine her, flinching as the cold instrument touched her warm flesh, "There's nothing wrong with me, I'm alright."

"Shh," the medical woman told her, trying to listen for a pulse, "This will only take a minute."

Having finished her checks, Dr. Rajpal took Sheila's temperature and put the back of her hand on the woman's neck. She was frowning, causing the gipsy to glare at her.

"I think you might be menopausal," the doctor concluded, "Have you been having hot flushes?"

"Well yes, now that you mention it I have," Sheila admitted, startled at the medic's conclusion, "Aren't I too young for all that malarkey?"

"Not necessarily," came the reply, "Given your medical history, I think you could be having it early. You'll be fine, you just need to ride it out and your body will settle down again in no time."

"Oh hell," Sheila cursed, "That's me done for then, the road to old age is upon me!"

"Nonsense," Doctor Rajpal scoffed, pulling out her prescription pad, "I'll give you something to take for the night sweats, but don't forget you're still able to get pregnant. You're Catholic aren't you?"

"Aye, so I am," Sheila confirmed, "But there's more chance of our gaffer getting up the duff than me, so there is, I won't be needing any advice on that thank you very much."

Indira blushed at the woman's forthrightness, she hadn't meant to imply that Sheila slept around, but it had been twelve months since their last meeting and she didn't know if there was a blossoming romance on the horizon. Tearing a sheet of paper off the pad, she handed it to Sheila.

"I have to get going," Indira told her, gently rising to her feet "I still have others to see today, but can I pop back in a couple of days to talk to you about smoking? Please?"

Sheila waved a hand flippantly, "Sure you can, but don't blame me if I'm busy, I have all sorts to do."

The doctor hurried away, all the time thinking about Sheila Hannigan's heartbeat.

Later on, as she went about her business, Sheila bumped into Danger McDougall on his way to the practice circuit. He was dressed casually in a check shirt and jeans, but looked noticeably more fashionable nowadays, an influence that most certainly came from Simone.

"Have you seen Doc Rajpal?" Sheila asked, coming straight to the point, "Is everything alright?"

"Clean bill of health," the stuntman grinned, thrusting his hands deep into his pockets, "She says my leg has healed well and my new French diet means I've become a bit leaner, which can only be a good thing."

"Oh, that's grand," Sheila nodded sincerely, "And what about Simone? Fit as a fiddle?"

"Erm, I think you'd better ask her," Mr. McDougall sighed, trying hard to hide his bubbling pride, "Oh crikey, I can't keep it to myself! She's having a baby! I'm going to be a father!"

Sheila stood transfixed as she heard the wonderful news, "Oh, I'm so happy for you both, come here and give me a big kiss you soft lad. Now where's that beautiful woman of yours?"

"I'm here," Simone flushed, stepping up behind the gipsy, "Sheila, you're going to be a godmother!"

It took a few hours before the implications of Simone Martin's announcement sunk in. The couple had naturally asked their best friend to be godmother to their child, but Sheila wasn't sure whether she really wanted that kind of responsibility. Besides, it would tie her to the circus, if she had duties to the newborn child. She could hardly go off and leave after becoming attached.

Sitting alone, mulling over the events of the day, Sheila broke down in tears. It had been an emotional rollercoaster kind of day, hearing that she was past her prime and now the news of Simone's baby. Nobody had stopped to think about how she would feel, becoming Aunty Sheila, not a thought to how the Irishwoman might be hurting inside over not having her own child to hold. And soon, maybe two or three years down the line, it would all be too late. She would be old and alone.

The psychic weighed up her options. She could leave, but truthfully she had burned all her bridges with the family back in Ireland and there was nowhere for her to go. She could stay with the circus until retirement age, becoming an unpaid helper and babysitter to her friend's child, quite a cherishing proposition in her mind, or she could finish what she'd set out to do and lay her skeletons to rest. With a bottle of red wine and a large bar of milk chocolate to her aid, Sheila finally drifted off to sleep, tossing and turning throughout the night as she subconsciously battled her demons.

Tap. Tap tap.

"Come in," Sheila shouted, hurriedly pulling a comb through her tangled mop of hair.

The door snapped open and Roland O'Hare appeared, his face ashen and his shoulders hunched.

"Can we talk Sheila?" he asked solemnly.

"Course we can," Sheila responded, genuinely concerned for the young lad, "Whatever's happened?"

"It's my Da, he's had some tests done. It's bad news, he's dying of heart disease."

Sheila gulped, she had no words but simply motioned for the ringmaster to sit down.

"Is this Doctor Rajpal's diagnosis?" she finally managed, "I mean, is she absolutely sure?"

"Aye," Roland nodded, "She drove him over to the hospital herself yesterday, what am I going to do Sheila? The old Devil's got less than a year to live, but for God's sake don't let on that you know."

"Your Da's a strong man, so he is," the Irishwoman cooed softly, putting her arm around Roland's shoulders, "He's so stubborn and he won't give up without a good fight, of that you can be sure."

Quite suddenly, without any warning, Roland O'Hare flung both arms around Sheila's neck and held her tight, "I'm so glad I've got you," he sobbed, "You're a rock Sheila Hannigan."

Gently peeling the young man off her, the gipsy let out a sigh, "I'll always be here for you, but we have to stay strong for your Da and make the time he's got left the best days of his life."

Later, having given the Chekovs a clean bill of health and prescribed painkillers for Ray Stubbs' aching back, Indira Rajpal headed towards 'Psychic Sheila's' caravan, intending to deliver a handful of leaflets outlining the warnings of heavy smoking and hopefully be treated to tea and biscuits in the gipsy's home. The doctor was dressed less formally that day, but still wore an air of professionalism as she tramped across the grass. Sheila had spotted her visitor leaving the strongman's trailer and had already filled the kettle, knowing full well that the medic would be parched.

"Ah, there you are," Doctor Rajpal huffed, stepping up into the caravan, "Time for a chat?"

"You don't need to lecture me," Sheila stiffened, "I gave up smoking last night."

"Really?" Indira enquired, "Just stopped suddenly eh? What brought that on?"

"Roly O'Hare," Sheila told her bluntly, "His son told me, figured I should get myself in better shape."

"Ah," the doctor nodded, open-mouthed.

"Is it true he's only got twelve months?"

Doctor Rajpal stiffened slightly, her professional head struggling to overpower her instincts to tell all.

"You know I can't discuss it with you Sheila," she eventually sighed, "Patient confidentiality and all that."

"Of course," the other woman replied tensely, "But in this community we're all family. Roly O'Hare's like a father to all the youngsters, despite his gruff manner, he'll be sorely missed."

"And what about you Sheila?" the doctor pressed, "Will you miss him?"

Sheila shrugged, her face open and honest, "No, I don't suppose I will."

As the days passed, Doctor Rajpal's health checks on the circus troupe came to an end. Apart from the sad test results from Mr. O'Hare's echocardiogram, there had been little to concern her, just a few aches and pains, plus of course the joyful news of Simone Martin's pregnancy. She did have a few concerns about Sheila Hannigan's stress levels however, and vowed to keep a watchful eye on the Irishwoman until it was time for the performing artists to move on. Indira was well aware that Sheila was haunted by ghosts from her past but she knew no specific details, nor just how far back those concerns went. Of course, she did wonder whether the gipsy had any close attachments to the men of the community. She'd heard Jake Collins referring to Sheila as 'Princess' in passing, and it was obvious that Roland O'Hare had dashed straight over to 'Psychic Sheila's' caravan the minute he'd heard the bad news about his father's illness. Still, it all added up to professional curiosity, or so the doctor told herself, hoping that she could see Sheila's spirits lifted before they packed up and left.

"Is there anything we can do to make the old man more comfortable?" Sheila asked on Doctor Rajpal's third visit that week, "I mean, would a healthier diet help? Or should he just enjoy a little bit of everything?"

"Why the sudden concern?" Indira asked, lifting her perfectly plucked eyebrows, "I've given Roland some information about what to expect and I'm sure he'd be glad of your help cooking some nutritious meals."

"That's just it," Sheila shot back, "I want to help Roland. His Da's a cantankerous old Devil but I wouldn't wish him any pain. If I can make things easier for them both, I will."

The doctor rubbed Sheila Hannigan's arm and smiled, "You're a good woman Sheila, they're very lucky to have you around. Living this kind of Romany lifestyle as you all do, it's not going to be easy convincing Roly to go into hospital when the time comes but…"

"No, he should be here, amongst his own kind," Sheila murmured softly, "God only knows that's what all circus folk would want. It wouldn't be right to let him die in a clinical hospital full of strangers."

Indira tensed, she would refrain from getting too closely involved, despite what her instincts told her.

"Here's my number," she told Sheila, taking a slip of blue paper from her jacket, "If ever you or anyone else need my advice, please call. Cardiology isn't my area of expertise but I can offer practical solutions. Now, I'd better get going, I've promised to bring my children to the Big Top tonight. See you later?"

'Psychic Sheila' found it difficult to concentrate on her client's readings that afternoon, as her mind kept wandering to Roly's heart condition and Simone's pregnancy. Both pieces of news had shocked her but they each had a completely different impact. Sheila felt slightly guilty that the thought of life without the circus gaffer would be more bearable, and Roland was more than capable of filling his father's shoes, but her heart wept for the young man who was so attached to his only surviving parent. As for Simone and Danger McDougall, well, she never doubted that the pair would make wonderful parents, sadly all the worry was whether she could fulfil their expectations of her as the child's godmother.

"Do you see anything?" the sixty-year old housewife asked nervously, "Should I expect any serious illness? It's my Reggie you see, I'm so worried about him."

Psychic Sheila forced her attention back to the swirling clouds in her crystal ball, the orange was fading and a purple mist now appeared before her eyes.

"No, Mrs. Cartwright," she replied steadily, "It's just a minor ailment, he'll be as right as rain in a week."

"Oh, thank heaven," the woman sighed, opening an old brown leather purse, "I'm so relieved."

"Have you recently bought a new car?" Sheila asked suddenly, taking the woman's proffered note and glancing back at the object in front of her. She waited until the puzzled pensioner nodded before adding, "It's the car that has the problem, Mrs. Cartwright, not your dog."

And there it was, a momentary lapse, worrying about her circus friends and then all the psychic powers came flooding back. Sheila knew that she had chosen the right vocation in life, or rather, it had chosen her but sometimes it didn't do to see the future, not when it concerned those close to you.

Closing the door after her last reading at five o'clock, Sheila Hannigan pulled off her headscarf and made a pot of tea. She still had a couple of hours before the main evening show and she intended to spend it clearing her mind and making herself look glamorous. It wouldn't do to reflect too deeply on things she couldn't change, Sheila mused, but there was no harm in looking on the bright side and hoping that the future might be brighter. She still held a cupboard full of demons in a dark corner of her memory but she wasn't quite ready to clear those particular cobwebs just yet. No, they'd have to stay in the dark until the time was right but, given the events of the past couple of days, the gipsy began to wonder if the time for retribution might be growing closer. Life was full of unexpected twists, she told herself, and eventually karma would turn about face and right all the wrongs of her youth.

The six o'clock news showed half asleep musician Bob Geldof talking about famine relief for Ethiopia. He looked dishevelled and the clothes on his back were crumpled, causing Sheila to frown intensely at the screen, muttering under her breath.

"Well, would you look at that, anyone would think you'd never ironed a shirt Bob, and that hair needs a paddle brush through it, so it does."

"Are you after talking to yourself again?" a deep Irish voice called through the open caravan window, "I swear to God you're going mad Sheila Hannigan."

Climbing up on to the side bunk in a most unladylike manner, Sheila scrambled up to the window and poked her head out, "You cheeky rascal Roland O'Hare, I can do what the feck I want in my own home so I can."

"Does that include entertaining young men?" he grinned, "Or are you saving yourself?"

"Don't be daft," Sheila blushed, "How many times do I have to tell you? Anyway, you've soon cheered up, have you had a good chat with your Da?"

"I certainly have," Roland replied, lowering his voice, "I have to accept that he won't be around for much longer, so we're going to make every minute count."

"Good, I'm glad to hear it," she replied, genuinely touched, "Now get yourself moving. Your Da's still well enough to tan your hide and you should be in the tent getting ready!"

"See you later," the cheeky chap winked, "I'll blow you a kiss from the ring."

Sheila chuckled and closed the window sighing. Roland had just made her heart melt.

Putting the final touches to her outfit with some coloured bangles and bright beads, Sheila Hannigan looked herself over carefully in the mirror. Despite Doctor Rajpal's comments about the menopause, the psychic didn't think she looked too bad for her age, just a bit overweight and out of condition. Maybe it wasn't too late for her to find love, although Sheila hardly remembered what a fluttering heartbeat felt like these days, let alone anything physical. There had been someone, a very long time ago when she was just seventeen but he had broken all of his promises and there had been no flicker of romance since. Sheila knew that life would become very lonely, as she inevitably watched her friends find love, but there was something she needed to do before letting that special someone in.

Struggling with her urge to smoke, Sheila set off towards the Big Top with a couple of Sherbet Dips in her pocket, more to satisfy the craving to put something in her mouth than anything. She figured that the taste of the sugar and liquorice combined would satisfy her until supper time but she intended to kick the habit for good. Roland O'Hare's illness had taken care of any qualms.

"Sheila," someone called as she made her way up to the back tier of seats, "Over here."

The gipsy turned to see Indira Rajpal waving at her from a nearby row.

"Hello," she yelled back over the loud hum of chattering voices, "Lovely to see you."

The doctor was accompanied by a very tall and handsome man and two identical children.

"This is Sonny, my husband," Indira explained, raising her voice, "And my twins."

Sheila smiled and raised a hand to the family, but then motioned towards her seat, "Better sit down, the show will start in a few minutes. Glad you could make it."

Moving away, she reflected once again on how perfect the lives of those around her were, something that was becoming increasingly hard to bear.

The show that night was spectacular. Simone Martin in particular was on fine form, perhaps buoyed by her recent good news, and the knife-throwing act received a standing ovation. Sheila watched intensely, secretly looking for signs of a little pregnancy bump on the young woman's stomach, but whatever might have been there was hidden underneath a purple scallop-edged jacket. Simone's beloved had finished his own outdoor performance some time earlier, impressing the crowds with his leap through fire and other daring stunts and now, if you looked closely enough, Danger McDougall could just be seen at the edge of the huge backdrop curtain, waiting to present his lover with a huge bouquet of flowers and balloons.

Jake Collins had a particularly busy night, directing his workers to move props and set up the ring for each new act. He was pretty hands on too, Sheila noticed, helping to rig up the huge net that would serve as a safety barrier between the high-flying Chekovs and the ground below. Sergei and Luana wore matching outfits as usual, this time green and gold, adding instant glamour as they bounced into the ring. Sheila had no hard feelings towards the couple, it was none of her business if they wanted to pretend to be just a little more exotic than they actually were, and she admired the way in which they handled the trapeze, as though it were the most natural thing in the world.

Just as Ray Stubbs came to stand before the audience, the resident clowns rode in on tiny tricycles, tying the strongman in knots with a length of red rope held between them. Around and around they rode until the huge man was as tightly wound up as some giant cobweb. Sheila howled with laughter as Raymond pretended to roar with rage, the tears rolling down the side of her face.

Later, as the act came to a close, Punch and Judy Robinson entered the ring again. Now in disguise, with thick black beards covering the lower part of their faces. It was such a farce, and the crowd loved it, shouting to Ray that the cheeky clowns were behind him and telling him to look out. It was just then, as the strongman gave chase to Punch, that Sheila saw a flash of crimson out of the corner of her eye. Indira Rajpal was getting up to leave, her beautiful pashmina flowing behind her and causing great distress to those seated nearby. They were telling her to sit down, or to get out of the way. The woman looked flustered but, from where she was sitting, Sheila couldn't see the doctor's face closely enough to tell if there was some problem and presumed that the woman simply needed to use the toilet.

Ten minutes later, with the Great Rolando introducing another act, there was still no sign of Indira Rajpal. Sheila feared that there may be a long queue to use the facilities and if that were the case a good deal of the show would be missed. She decided, purely from the goodness of her heart, to investigate.

It wasn't hard to locate Mrs. Rajpal, her crimson sari and matching shawl positively illuminated her and there actually weren't many people outside during show time, therefore within a few seconds Sheila was heading towards a tree at the rear of the showground. Puffs of smoke curled upwards from a cigarette.

"So there you are," Sheila announced, talking to the Indian woman's back, "You certainly don't practice what you preach do you?"

"What?"

"Smoking," Sheila tutted, "After the hard time you gave me!"

Indira Rajpal slowly shuffled her feet until she was facing Sheila, her face streaked with tears.

"No I don't," she whispered, "And it's a disgusting habit."

"Hey now, what's all this?" Sheila soothed sympathetically, "Why the tears? Don't tell me you want to run away with the circus now?"

The joke fell flat and Indira began sobbing uncontrollably, her body trembling from head to toe.

"Come on," the gipsy murmured, "It can't be that bad. Who's upset you? Is it because of the bad news you've had to deliver to Roly this week?"

The woman shook her head, "No, I'm used to that in my profession."

"So what then?"

"It was those clowns," the doctor wept, "When they came in wearing those dreadful beards."

Sheila bit her lip, resisting the urge to laugh out loud, "Look I know they look ridiculous but there's no need to get upset over it. Did it scare you? I know a lot of people have nightmares about clowns."

Indira Rajpal sunk down to the ground, resting her back against the trunk of the tree and then began dabbing at her face with a clean tissue.

"Sheila can you keep a secret?" she whispered.

The gipsy nodded and eased her ample rump onto the grass beside the doctor, "I certainly can."

It was then that Indira Rajpal confided something that she'd kept to herself for a lifetime.

"Growing up in India, we had a comfortable life, that was until my father lost his job at the tax office. They told him that people were talking, about me you see, causing him to lose face amongst his colleagues," Indira began, pausing for breath as she gathered her thoughts.

"I don't understand," Sheila frowned, "Why were they talking about you?"

"When I was born, I had a very rare genetic condition," the doctor went on, "Causing my parents great embarrassment. I was kept indoors and only allowed out with a veil covering my face."

Sheila blinked, wondering what kind of disfigurement could have suddenly disappeared, as Indira was a beautiful young woman these days, there was no mistaking that.

"I was covered in hair," the Indian woman explained, seeing the confusion on her confidante's face, "All around my cheekbones, on my chin, just like a man, thick dark horrible hair."

Sheila opened her mouth to say something but quickly realised that this was not the moment to express her surprise and continued to sit, waiting for more.

"It just never stopped growing," Indira said softly, her eyes still staring at the ground by her feet, "Of course, we lived in such a small town that my father couldn't keep it a secret forever. The minute my mother took me to the hospital, everyone wanted to see her freak of a child, the hairy girl."

Sheila coughed gently to signal she wanted to speak, "How awful, you poor thing."

"Well, everyone started making fun of my father and said it was the curse of the Devil that had caused my disfigurement, and he believed them. As soon as I was school age, he packed me off to a travelling show where I had to earn my living as a bearded lady. It was truly horrendous Sheila, I wanted to die."

"But you're fine now," the psychic pointed out, "How come?"

"Luckily I met my husband, who happens to be a doctor and medical scientist," Indira told her, "He took me to Switzerland to have treatment to remove the hair and it worked, after that we fell in love."

Sheila smiled, "And now?"

"I still have to take hormone tablets and go back to the clinic every six months but apart from a slight five o'clock shadow, I'm almost normal."

Sheila Hannigan sighed and took the doctor's hand.

"Look love," she lectured, "We're dealt a hand in life and there's nothing we can do about it. God gives us challenges for a reason. If you hadn't been in that freak show, you wouldn't have met your husband, and you wouldn't have those two beautiful children would you?"

Indira Rajpal chuckled and hugged the gipsy tightly, "You're very wise, you know Sheila, I wish I'd met you years ago. You're right, I should be thankful for the here and now."

"That's a girl," Sheila grinned, pulling the doctor to her feet, "Now let's go and see if we can find Punch and Judy. We've got a couple of beards to burn."

Chapter Eight

Jake Collins

It was September. The circus troupe had travelled out of the city and down to the South coast, where fresh salty sea air and the sound of squawking gulls were in abundance. Pure white sand dunes filled the landscape to the left whilst a busy seaside town sprawled to the right, the perfect location for the Big Top to draw their customers from the late summer tourists and residents alike. Of course, the travelling folk were pleased with their new environment too, as the choice of eateries ranged from fish and chip shops to high-end restaurants, with the mid-range option being half a dozen taverns serving homemade fresh meals and locally brewed beer. However, there appeared to be one member of the group who was reluctant to sample the delicacies of the town and Sheila Hannigan was determined to find out why.

Jake Collins had been in a dire mood since the moment of their arrival and had even insisted that the rigging crew begin work immediately, despite it being close to lunchtime and them having a full day ahead before the tent needed to be up. He stood barking orders as Roly O'Hare looked on from his caravan. He never interfered with the tent master's decisions when it came to setting up as Jake was a master when it came to judging weather conditions and timing, therefore he stood back watching as the crew heaved and hammered, spreading the gigantic canvas onto the field before using the crane to pull it up into position. Elsewhere, there were other slightly less important issues taking place.

On the afternoon of their arrival at the new site, Sheila had accidentally broken one of her cupboard doors from yanking it too hard and the offending item now lay in a sorry state, hanging from the hinges. She had already called on Ray Stubbs to help her but unfortunately the strongman had admitted that he'd have more luck with a pair of knitting needles than a hammer, suggesting that instead he would go and find Jake Collins as he knew him to be qualified as a master joiner.

"Well, I never knew that," Sheila chirped as Ray turned to leave, "Maybe he can make me some new door fronts instead of fixing the old ones…."

"You can certainly ask him," the heavily set man agreed, rubbing his chin thoughtfully, "Although he's probably the busiest bloke around here these days. Today is a fine example, he could have left setting up until later but no, there he is working like a Trojan."

Sheila watched Ray leave but stood with a twinkle in her eye, Jake would help out, of that she had no doubt. After all, she would turn on her Irish charm.

Sometime later, having finally agreed to let his workers take a well-deserved break, Jake Collins sat drinking tea in Sheila's caravan. Having inspected the damaged unit, he agreed that it was high time to replace the cupboard doors and was more than willing to help.

Sheila sat at the table opposite and watched the burly man animatedly outline his idea, taking in his closely cropped hair, dragon tattoo and unusual gold earring. Jake appeared to like the thought of doing a favour for Sheila that wasn't part of his usual humdrum routine and he even knew a good kitchen salesroom outside of town where he could buy new doors for a knockdown price.

"I didn't know you knew the area?" Sheila commented as she refilled Jake's mug from the teapot, "Are you from these parts?"

"No!" the tent master spluttered, "I just happened to notice the kitchen salesroom as we drove in. Now what colour are you thinking Sheila? Maybe a nice light wood?"

"Isn't pine all the rage these days?" she asked, wondering why her guest looked like a rabbit caught in headlights, "With brass handles to match my bits and bobs."

"Fair enough," Jake agreed, "I'll be sure to get you the best price and fit them before we move on again."

Sheila smiled gratefully, watching the man's hoop earring jingle up and down as he spoke. It was an unusual piece of jewellery, she thought, with a little skull and crossbones attached to the ring, not something she'd ever seen up close before.

"Will I pay you now?" she enquired, reaching across for her purse.

"Let's see what kind of deal I can get," Jake told her, "Then we'll talk about money Princess."

The following day, Sheila was booked up with readings for most of the afternoon and didn't notice Jake Collins driving his truck off the site and out of town. However, as she opened the door for her last customer, 'Psychic Sheila' did see him coming back, quite unusually wrapped up for the warm sunny day that it was, dressed in a heavy parka coat and peaked cap. He was walking with his head down and appeared to have half a dozen large boxes in the back of his vehicle.

"Those must be my new doors!" she grinned.

"Sorry?" the customer asked, thinking that Sheila was talking to her, "Did you say something?"

"No, dear," the gipsy said, still keeping her eyes fixed on Jake, "Not a thing."

Watching the muscular man unload the boxes one by one, Sheila Hannigan felt a pang of excitement. New cupboards doors would transform her kitchen area and give the caravan a much needed revamp. Maybe I could even spend some more of my savings and buy new curtains too, she pondered. Sheila didn't want much out of life, and this mobile home on wheels was her pride and joy. She wondered how she could repay Jake for his kindness, as it was obvious he wouldn't charge her for his labour, but for the moment Sheila pushed that thought to the back of her mind and focussed on putting her crystal ball away.

That night, the Big Top was packed to the rafters, so to speak, and Sheila had to push her way through excited children and gossiping adults to get to her reserved seat, sitting down just minutes before the curtain opened to reveal a resplendent Roland O'Hare standing proud in his ringmaster's outfit. Even though she watched the same performers, night after night, their acts only varying at season's end, Sheila Hannigan felt a sense of pride every time the audience cheered and waved. Tonight was no different, although she was also keeping an eye out for Jake Collins, hoping that he would have some news on his start date for the refurbishment. Sheila wasn't disappointed, for as she made her way back from the ice-cream seller at half-time, Jake was standing head and shoulders above the crowd looking for her.

"There's my Princess," he announced, "Just wondering if I could start on your units tomorrow?"

"Well of course you can!" Sheila told him cheerfully, "I can't wait to see my new doors."

"Great, if you don't mind I'll come over at seven for a few hours, you know, before I start my real work."

Sheila nodded and carefully licked at a trickle of ice-cream that was running down her hand, "That'll be grand, although don't be frightened if I'm still in my nightie!"

Jake chuckled and motioned towards the line of people moving back towards their seats, having filled up on various treats and beverages, "You'd better get back to your place, while you can Princess."

"Oh feck," she chuckled, "Don't want to miss the show. See you tomorrow Jake, and thanks."

Jake Collins stood admiring the Irishwoman's rear as she bustled away in her velour tracksuit, wondering why it was that Sheila Hannigan remained relentlessly single, despite the growing population of eligible males within the circus family. It amused him that she never seemed lonely but was always the life and soul of the group. He wondered what his mother would make of Sheila, should they ever have the fortune to meet, although he was pretty sure that both of his parents would frown upon Sheila's constant stream of cursing. Jake wondered if fitting the new cabinet fronts would give him the opportunity to ask the mysterious gipsy out on a date, although he was scared stiff that she already had her eyes and claws well and truly fixed upon someone much younger and more handsome.

He tucked his head around the canvas sheeting and strained his neck to where Sheila was now sitting. Following her gaze, Jake could see that he'd been right all along, although he hadn't realised to what extent until now. Sheila was nibbling at the biscuit cone of her cornet and smiling at someone in the distance, an expression that oozed with love and emotion, and most definitely directed towards the tall, dark and muscular figure of ringmaster Roland O'Hare.

Knowing that Jake would be arriving early the next day, Sheila was up and pegging washing on her line when he arrived. The aroma of fresh coffee permeated the air of her neat little caravan and the contents of her cupboards sat piled up on the kitchenette table.

"Well, well, you're highly organised this morning Princess," he announced, pulling a screwdriver from his tool-belt, "I'll take the old doors off first, and we'll go from there."

Sheila pushed back a lock of hair and looked him up and down, "Have you had breakfast yet?"

"I certainly have," Jake told her, setting to work without delay, "But a mug of that coffee would go down a treat. And Sheila?"

She blinked, the sound of her name alerting her to something new, something different.

"While I work, you can tell me your life story and why it is that you're still single."

The next couple of hours passed uneventfully. Sheila made up a cock and bull story about never finding the right man and Jake Collins listened intently, taking in every word. It did concern Sheila, just ever so slightly that she was such a good liar, as contrary to popular belief she always told the truth about what she saw in people's past and future, her own life however was a place where nobody was allowed in.

"So you see," she concluded, after spinning a yarn about being too picky when it came to love, "I've just never met the love of my life. Although, I'm sure there's some fecker out there waiting for me."

"Would you go out on a date with me?" Jake spluttered, surprising himself as the words tumbled out, "I mean, if you'd like to we could go out for a bite to eat or to the pictures."

Sheila sucked in her breath, knowing that this moment had been on the horizon for months, and slowly let it out again as she thought about the question.

"Why the hell not," she answered, trying to sound as casual as she could.

Jake carried on unscrewing the cupboard doors, his ears turning red as took in Sheila's response.

"There's a nice pub in town that does lovely steak and chips," she continued.

"No, not there," Jake told her, "I'll take you out of town tomorrow lunchtime, away from prying eyes."

As the truck travelled along the by-pass and then through a series of small villages, Sheila couldn't help but wonder why Jake wanted to keep their rendez-vous such a closely guarded secret. After all, both Roly and Simone had seen them leaving the campsite together and no doubt it would only be a matter of time before tongues would begin to wag. She didn't care, it was high time Sheila Hannigan had a bit of attention. As they pulled into the car park of a small tavern, Sheila noted that there were no other vehicles around and the place looked a bit tired and dated with paint peeling off the rear walls.

"Have you been here before?" she asked, climbing down from her seat, "It looks deserted."

Jake shrugged, "It'll be cosy Princess, don't you worry we'll have a nice lunch."

Inside, a wizened old man sat hugging half a pint of beer while the landlord leaned against a barstool studying the racing news in his paper. He barely glanced up as the newcomers made their way inside, although a scraggly dog with dirty fur got up from its place by the fire and sniffed at them.

Jake stooped to ruffle the dog's fur and then turned his attention to the publican, "Do you have a lunch menu we could look at?"

The man eyed them warily, closed his newspaper and then coughed, "Food? We haven't served a meal in twenty years. Best bet is down the by-pass, plenty of places to eat on the seafront."

Sheila let out a sigh, she was beginning to feel rather hungry and time was getting on, but Jake was approaching the bar and deciding which of the real ales to order.

"What would you like?" he asked Sheila, oblivious to the exasperated look on her face.

"I'll have an orange juice please," she mumbled, looking at her watch, "And a packet of beef and onion crisps."

Jake took the hint and flushed, a pink tinge rising in his cheeks, "Some meal eh?"

"Well, we don't have time to go back into town to eat now," Sheila sighed, "I have to be back by two."

Her companion nodded, and carried their drinks to a small table by the fireplace, "I'm sorry Princess."

"What was wrong with eating at one of the local pubs anyway, or the café?" she asked tensely.

"I just, didn't want to," Jake sighed, "Let's leave it at that."

Despite their disastrous first date, Jake continued his work on Sheila's cupboards until the job was completed a few days later. Much to her delight, the joiner had made her a fold-away ironing board that slotted into a neat space and added shiny new handles to all of the units.

"How much do I owe you for your work?" Sheila quizzed, inspecting the receipt for the wooden doors and counting out the correct notes, "I need to give you something for your trouble."

Jake Collins shook his head, causing the little skull and crossbones on his earring to flicker up and down, 'I don't want your money, but how about a second date, to make up for the last one?"

Sheila folded her arms and scowled, "Let me think about it Jake."

As the week passed, Sheila began to feel guilty about taking her friend's workmanship for granted. Every time she entered the caravan, it was like a brand new experience, such a difference had the new pine kitchen doors made. If the only way to repay Jake was to go out with him then so be it, she told herself, besides she really had taken a shine to him. Therefore, as soon as she had some free time, Sheila Hannigan took a short stroll into town to take a look at some of the menus on offer. Being mainly a tourist resort, the more expensive restaurants displayed their meals on boards outside, enabling potential customers to see both the selection of food on offer and the prices that they could expect to pay.

Sheila took out her spectacles and read down the list from the first place she came to. There seemed to be good choice of both English and foreign foods but she wasn't sure if her budget would stretch to a bottle of wine in this particular place, as it seemed rather too dear. The next establishment had a cosier feel and the menu was Italian, with drinks ranging from very cheap to reasonably expensive. She peered through the window and took in the crisp linen tablecloths and smartly dressed waiters.

"Grand," she told herself, "I'll book us a table in here."

However, on returning to the circus, when Sheila raced to tell Jake Collins what she'd done, it was with a heavy heart that she listened to his ungrateful response.

"I'm sorry Princess," he complained, "I thought I'd made myself clear, I don't want to go to any of the restaurants around here. If you want to go, you'll have to find somebody else to go with, otherwise cancel it and I'll take you somewhere out of town. That's my final word on the matter."

Sheila walked away feeling both confused and irate. Inside her head there were alarm bells ringing. Something wasn't right, she didn't need her psychic instincts to tell her that but she couldn't for the life of her fathom out what it was. The only reasonable conclusion that she could come to was that Jake Collins had a woman somewhere and was afraid of being seen out and about with Sheila. Well, if that were the case, she concluded, it was his loss. Sheila Hannigan didn't play second fiddle to anyone.

As the week drew to a close, O'Hare's circus family began to think about their next move. It wasn't far, not more than fifty miles or so, but the location was to be inland which dulled their spirits after having spent a week with fresh sea air in their lungs. Naturally, with such an array of excellent eateries on their doorstep, talk turned towards a celebratory meal before leaving and it was Sheila who offered to book it. She had felt slightly embarrassed about having to cancel her meal for two at the Italian restaurant, the staff had been so welcoming and so, as a gesture of goodwill, she booked one large group meal for her friends. The party would pretty much fill the dining area without other clientele, as almost everyone wanted to attend. The exception was Jake Collins.

Therefore, on their last night in town, as the group headed off for a late meal after their final performance, Jake Collins was nowhere to be seen. Sheila could see a light on in his trailer as she glanced over after locking her caravan door, but no sign that the tent master intended on joining them. The invitation had been issued the day before but had been met with nothing more than a shake of the head, so she wouldn't push her luck and left him well alone.

"What have you done to Jake?" asked Ray Stubbs asked as he walked beside Sheila to the seafront, "It's not like him to miss out on a hot meal."

"Oh, don't ask," she tutted, "He's been acting strange ever since we got here, I reckon he's got a woman tucked away somewhere."

The strongman ran his fingers through his short coarse hair and thought for a moment, "But I thought you and Jake were, you know, starting to get close."

'Don't be daft," Sheila laughed, trying to convince herself more than her friend, "What on earth gave you that idea? He's just been good enough to fix my kitchen doors, that's all, you daft devil."

That night, the Italian restaurant was filled with laughter. Even Roly O'Hare seemed to enjoy himself, despite having to curb the quantity of alcohol he ingested, and he rose to make a toast.

"To all of you," the gaffer cheered, "You make me proud."

Glasses were raised and the chatter recommenced, followed by plates of meatballs and pasta being served alongside garlic bread and Parmesan.

"What kind of cheese is that?" Punch Robinson asked, examining the finely grated mound of shavings.

Sheila gave him a nudge under the table, "It's from Italy, the traditional topping to put on your dinner. And don't think I didn't see you pocket those salt and pepper pots either."

The little man reluctantly slid the cruet set back onto the tablecloth and grinned, "Old habits die hard."

"Well, just so you know," Sheila warned, "I've got my beady eye on the pair of you."

"What's up?" asked Danger McDougall, having witnessed the sharp looks from across the table, "Are you causing trouble Punch Robinson?"

The dwarfed man shrugged, a grin appearing on his face, "Just offering to clean Sheila's caravan windows tomorrow, if someone will lend me a ladder."

There was raucous laughter around the table as the group envisaged the three foot man trying to do a job which anyone else could manage just by standing on the ground, and a barrage of hilarious jokes and ribbing followed.

Inevitably, a wonderful night was had by all. The food was excellent, several tomato stained shirts being a testament to the delicious sauces, and a fair amount of wine was consumed, and to top it all off, Roly O'Hare offered to pay when the bill came, showing his workers that there was a softer side to his nature after all. On the walk home, Sheila made a point of personally thanking him.

"Much appreciated Roly," she told him, "I've really enjoyed myself tonight."

"You know what Sheila?" he replied, wheezing slightly as they made their way back to the camp, "I have too, so I have. Lord only knows how long I've got left, but I'm going to enjoy the time that I've got. By the way, what's up with Jake tonight? I thought he'd be up for a good feed."

The gipsy shrugged, she wished that she knew what was wrong with the tent master, "I have no idea, that man's a law unto himself."

Turning in for the night, Sheila stood watching her friends making their way to their respective homes. There had been great camaraderie tonight, she reflected, it wasn't often that they had chance to go out for a big meal all together, and over the coming months there was no doubt that things would change. Roly O'Hare would inevitably become weaker as his heart condition worsened and the arrival of Simone's baby would bring a new generation into the fold, but for herself, Sheila reflected, life would be the same. Unless, of course, she did something to change it.

Sheila closed the door and set about making herself a mug of cocoa before bed. The daily newspaper lay on her kitchen table unread, the headlines filled with information about rioting gangs in the country's capital city. She shuddered, glad that they have moved to the coast, away from any danger, although her heart went out to the many businesses and homeowners who had lost a fortune due to the uncontrollable sieges on the built-up housing estates.

Flicking to the centre pages with her warm mug in one hand, something caught Sheila's eye. It was article about a local man and there was a strange familiarity to the photograph that accompanied it.

"It has been ten years since local man Johnny Coleman disappeared," she read aloud, having to squint at the print without her glasses, "And police still have no clue as to what happened. On the morning of September 6th 1975, the man's shoes and coat were found washed up on the local beach, leading his family and friends to believe that he may have drowned. Mr. Coleman was a master joiner by trade and was well-known in the area as a friendly and likeable member of the community. He is survived by his wife, Yvonne."

Sheila quickly rummaged around for her spectacles and looked closely at the photo underneath the article. It showed a handsome man in his early forties with long curly hair and a muscular frame. She didn't recognise him exactly, but there was definitely something about the man that made her look again. Suddenly realising what the familiarity was, Sheila reached in a cupboard and pulled out a magnifying glass. She positioned it over the man's face and peered down.

"Well, I'll be damned," Sheila cursed, finding it hard to believe that her eyes weren't deceiving her, "He's still wearing that same skull and crossbones earring, no wonder Jake didn't want to be seen in town!"

The psychic sat thinking on her bunk, the cocoa going cold as she pondered. The implications of exposing Jake Collins were enormous but Sheila's sympathy lay with the man's poor wife. Having her husband disappear like that must have been devastating for the poor woman.

Sheila Hannigan didn't sleep well at all that night. She got up from her warm bed on a couple of occasions, simply to gaze at the photograph in the newspaper and then to reread the short article. Now that she'd had time to study the picture closely, Sheila could see that the man was Jake Collins. Admittedly, Jake no longer sported long curly locks but the eyes were unmistakeable, even though the photo was in black and white, and that chiselled jawbone was the same one that she'd secretly admired on their drive out to that little village pub. The strange skull and bones earring was the final nail in the coffin, so to speak, and left no doubt in Sheila's mind that Johnny Coleman was here, working in the circus under an assumed name.

The following morning, preparations for the move were underway, everyone securing their trailers and caravans ready for the journey and equipment being loaded onto the flatbed trucks. Sheila took down her ornaments, as was customary at the end of each stay, and packed them into a large cardboard box for safety. She didn't intend to suffer breakages on the journey at any cost.

Pulling a couple of Sherbet Dips out of the kitchen drawer, she wondered what she could do to keep herself occupied during the trip. Danger McDougall hadn't travelled with her since starting his relationship with Simone and although this wasn't going to be a long trip, Sheila wondered if she might get bored. In a moment of sudden inspiration, she trotted over to Raymond Stubbs' trailer, picking up the previous day's newspaper from where it lay beside her bed.

"Is there any chance you've got a book I can borrow for the journey Ray?" Sheila asked politely, "You know how I need something to occupy my mind."

Ray Stubbs pointed to a small pile of books on his table, "I've been managing quite well lately you know, I've almost finished those."

Sheila smiled. Under her tuition, the strongman had increased his reading skills remarkably in just a matter of weeks although his choice of books wasn't exactly what she'd been expecting.

"Wind in the Willows," she read, picking the first book off the top of the pile, "My word, you are doing well."

"Is that for me?" Ray asked, gesturing towards the newspaper that the gipsy still held in her hand.

Sheila flushed and opened it to the centre page, "Look here, do you recognise this man?"

Raymond shook his head on seeing the photo and then slowly read the print, his huge forefinger tracing the words along the page as he did so, "Johnny Coleman, no, never heard of him."

"What about the initials?" Sheila hinted, "J.C., the same as Jake Collins."

The strongman squinted, not fully understanding.

"Look at the earring," Sheila sighed, "And imagine Johnny Coleman without long hair."

Ray suddenly realised what his friend was implying and took a closer look at the photograph.

"Are you sure Sheila?"

"Of course I'm fecking sure," she groaned, "It's bleeding obvious."

"Well, there's one way to find out for sure." The burly man grinned, "Come on."

Sheila had no idea where they were going as she tried to keep pace with Raymond's heavy frame as he lumbered across the grass. By the time they reached Jake Collins's toolbox where the tent master had left it near the flattened Big Top, she was both out of breath and bewildered.

"He'll be back from his coffee break in a minute," Ray warned, "We'll have to be quick. Keep a look out."

"What on earth are you up to?" Sheila chuckled, feeling like a naughty schoolgirl.

"Well," her companion explained, picking up the heavy wooden mallet that lay on top of Jake's toolbox, "There's something about master joiners that you need to know."

"And what's that?" Sheila giggled, putting her hands on her hips as she kept a close eye on matters.

Ray clenched the handle of the mallet between his knees and put one hand either side of the mallet head.

"Master joiners," he continued, "Do something quite unique, they hide their secrets in the tools of their trade, more specifically, they engrave them on the handle of their mallet."

Sheila stepped closer and inspected the tool in Ray's grasp, "I don't see anything on there."

"Aha," he announced, tugging at the mallet head, "That's the best part. They engrave the secret onto the tip of the handle, the part that fits into the head. That way it's hidden from view."

Sheila was amused, she'd never heard such an unlikely tale, "Are you pulling my leg Raymond Stubbs?"

Ray didn't answer as he was engaged in pulling the mallet head off which required strength and concentration in equal measure. With a final heave, the head flew off and Ray rolled backwards.

Sheila bent over laughing as the strongman lay on the grass with his legs in the air.

"Quick, help me up before anyone sees us," he gasped, struggling to his feet, the mallet handle now lying to one side in the mud, "Let's see what is says."

"Oh, you do the honours," Sheila chuckled, not really expecting to see anything.

Ray carefully rolled the piece of wood in his fingers, until he could make out the chiselled words.

"I FAKED MY OWN DEATH," he read aloud, "Blimey Sheila you were right."

"And you would have done the same if you'd been in a loveless marriage with a bitch of a wife trying to take you for every penny," a voice behind them growled, "Now if you don't mind I'll need my mallet."

The pair had been too engrossed in their findings to notice Jake Collins sneaking up behind them and now, rather red-faced, they apologised and walked away, leaving the tent master to his work and his thoughts.

Chapter Nine

The Tranters

It was a common sight amongst the circus folk to see two young children helping their father with his work. The boys in question were Dominic and Damon Tranter, a pair of rough and ready brothers who were always getting up to mischief with their wild shenanigans. Their father, Don, toiled under the direction of Jake Collins and classed himself as an all-rounder, that being that he was willing to labour, repair and replace anything at all that needed attending to. The boys were well-behaved enough when there were jobs for them to do but unfortunately they became bored easily, as young boys do, and it was at that point when the pranks began. It had been asked, at some point in a distant conversation, how the boys were being educated, what with travelling around the country as they did, but the response had been a simple one, their mother was teaching them at home.

Now, it has to be said, that Molly Tranter was what might be termed a rough diamond. She was from a long line of travellers, namely the traditional Romany kind, and spoke with a blunt forwardness that not everyone appreciated. On the other hand, Molly could be kind and funny, when she wanted to, and certainly worked as many hours as was humanly possible, both for her family and at the circus. Molly believed that she was educating her boys in the same way in which she had been schooled, to work your way up the ladder and try to earn money on the way. Of course, she taught them the basics in reading and writing but didn't have a clue where to start when it came to geography or maths and as a result the boys were lacking in general knowledge.

Sheila Hannigan tried her best to avoid Molly Tranter, although she would never have admitted it. She found the woman crass and loud, and despite them being in the same age bracket could never find a single topic to bring up in conversation. It was a strange situation, which deeply amused some of the other circus folk, as there were so many similarities between the two women that anyone looking in from outside would have expected them to be the best of friends. They both came from gipsy families and were used to a life on the road, both women had a rather flamboyant fashion sense and were slightly overweight and the pair also shared a habit of swearing constantly, although Sheila had been consciously trying to curb her language of late. There was something that gnawed at Sheila every time she happened to encounter Molly Tranter and it scared her that looking at the other gipsy was like looking in the mirror, except that the other woman had managed to bag herself a handsome husband and together they had produced two good-looking boys. Molly, in turn, was secretly jealous of Ms. Hannigan's freedom and popularity amongst her male co-workers, a trait that reminded Molly of her younger days. The only other significant difference between the two women was that Sheila was Irish and Molly was from the Northern English borderlands.

As the troupe set up at the next town, the weather began to turn cooler with night breezes and the occasional dark cloud. With children across the country being back at school, the performers were back to busy evenings and weekends, leaving midweek afternoons free to practice and get some well-earned rest.

It was on one of these lazy September afternoons that a stranger arrived at the camp.

Carefully locking his brown Ford Mondeo and adjusting his spectacles before setting off towards the Big Top, the tall and lanky man carried a clipboard and wore a sensible green corduroy jacket. Pairing the coat with tweed trousers, it was obvious to anyone watching that the gentleman was in the profession of education, either being a teacher or a school board official. Several men stopped work and watched as the stranger trod carefully across the field, trying desperately not to get his brogues muddy. There were also murmured voices as he knocked on the door of the first caravan that he came to, which just happened to belong to Sheila Hannigan.

"I say, good afternoon Madam," the man said, introducing himself in a rather nasal voice, "My name is Andrew Bassett and I'm looking for the Tranter family."

Sheila eyed the card that was being offered across, it read 'Education Authority' in bold letters.

"Tranter," she mumbled, shaking her head, "Can't say I know anybody of that name?"

"Really?" the man replied somewhat startled, "I have information to the contrary."

"Well, I'm sorry," Sheila sighed, starting to close her caravan door, "The information must be wrong.'

Peeping out from behind her net curtains, Sheila could see the bewildered man still standing outside her home. He was frowning intensely and writing something on his clipboard.

"Feck," she cursed, "I'm not having Molly Tranter blaming me for setting the school authorities on her."

She sighed heavily as Mr. Bassett finally walked away, this time in the direction of Ray Stubbs' home and wondered if she should run out and shout a word of warning but then relented.

"Why should I get myself all worked up?" she asked herself, "If Molly's been educating those boys properly then there should be no problem. I'll keep my nose out of other folks business."

It wasn't until later that Sheila got to hear the full story about Andrew Bassett's visit.

"Somebody must have reported us to the education people," Don Tranter was telling Jake as Sheila passed by on her way to the Big Top, "They seem to think the boys should be in school."

"Well, they do have a point I suppose…" Jake began.

"Nonsense," Don interrupted, "Molly gives those lads a good education, they can read better than me."

"Is there anything wrong?" Sheila asked casually, stepping closer.

"No, no, nothing at all," Don mumbled, half-heartedly, "Unless it was you that reported us?"

"Me?!" Sheila gulped, "Why on earth would I do that?"

"Sorry love," Don apologised, embarrassed at his outburst, "I know it wouldn't be you."

Sheila scurried inside the tent, annoyed at herself that she'd shown any concern, and sat down to watch the evening circus performance.

The following day, Mr. Bassett was back. He'd arrived early in the morning this time, whilst most of the circus folk were still in their caravans eating breakfast. Unlike the previous day, he now knew where to head and strode purposely towards the Tranter's home hoping, no doubt, to catch them unawares.

Sheila Hannigan was sitting on her doorstep drinking coffee and watched the scene unfold. She wasn't being intentionally nosey but, seeing as the Tranter's caravan was parked opposite her own, it was hard not to take notice. She could see that Andrew Bassett was wearing the same country gentleman's attire as he'd worn the previous day and wondered if it was standard practice for officials to dress in this way. It was almost as though he were trying to make his job seem less authoritative and more people friendly. Sheila took another sip from her large mug and looked on. Voices were muffled as Don Tranter opened his trailer door and his wife appeared to be very animated lounging in the doorway behind him.

It was only a few moments before Mr. Bassett tore a sheet of paper from his clipboard and handed it to Don Tranter, pointing his finger sternly as he did so. They were too far away for Sheila to hear clearly but she knew instinctively that there was trouble brewing. During the altercation there had been no sign of Dominic or Damon, leaving plenty of questions to form themselves in the psychic's mind. However, with the kerfuffle over for now, she returned inside and made another cup of coffee.

Later that morning, as Sheila Hannigan was sandwiching together two layers of a freshly baked chocolate cake with buttercream, there came a knock at her door. She quickly wiped her sticky fingers on a damp cloth and opened the door.

"Mam says can she borrow a needle?" Dominic Tranter bellowed loudly.

"Please," Sheila corrected, "Can she borrow a needle please?"

"Well can she?" the cheeky voice of younger brother Damon butted in, "She's hurt her finger and it's gone purple, she's worried the nail will fall off."

Sheila looked the boys up and down, they had holes in their denim dungarees and both children's hair stood up in tufts on the top of their heads. Dominic's shirt had been very badly repaired and the pocket was hanging off while Damon's shoes had a big hole in the toe.

"Wait there," Sheila muttered, cursing under her breath, those two young rascals had no manners at all but she knew exactly what Molly Tranter needed the needle for, it was an old housewife's tale that piercing the nail of a purple finger would release the trapped blood and save the fingernail.

"We'll bring it back, honest," Dominic promised, as Sheila handed him a sharp needle wrapped in cotton wool, "Just as soon as she's finished with it."

Sheila wrinkled her nose, "Don't bother, tell your mammy she can keep it, I have plenty more and I hope her finger gets better soon."

Watching the boys scurrying off across the field, the psychic wondered what Molly had been doing to damage her finger. She hoped that it was nothing to do with her children.

A couple of hours later, with the chocolate cake inside a plastic tub in her arms, Sheila headed over towards Roly O'Hare's trailer. She knew he'd be delighted with what she'd brought, his sweet tooth being the sick man's only pleasure these days, but felt a pang of guilt at not following doctor's orders. Indira Rajpal had been very specific about the types of food that Roly should be having, plenty of vegetables and fish amongst them, but Sheila just knew that a few slices of cake would perk him up no end. She didn't stay long, after all there was no love lost between her and the gaffer but Roly did seem genuinely appreciative of the cake and thanked Sheila warmly. She made her excuses to leave after ten minutes and walked back out into the sunshine.

A little way further across the field, Danger McDougall was revving his motorbike and watching fumes come out of the exhaust, so Sheila crept up behind him and tickled his ribs.

"Lord woman, you gave me a fright!" the Scouser exclaimed, switching off the engine, "Don't you know I've got a highly sensitive disposition?"

Sheila giggled, "Don't be daft, you're going to become a dad very shortly, so you'll have to have nerves of steel with all the nappy changing and crying."

The stuntman nodded and sighed contentedly, "You're right there Sheila, anyway what are you up to over this side in broad daylight? Shouldn't you be hunched over your crystal ball or something?"

She slapped him on the arm and rolled her eyes, "No customers until four today my lad. Anyway what's been going on over at the Tranter's?"

"Dunno," Danger McDougall shrugged, "I saw the truant officer leave and then there was a lot of shouting but I haven't seen Molly or Don all morning."

"Truant officer?" Sheila repeated slowly, widening her eyes, "I thought they were registered as being schooled at home."

The stuntman raised his arms in mock surrender, "Hey, don't shoot the messenger, it was just an observation."

"Interesting," Sheila muttered, "I wonder what's really going on."

Trampling back across the damp grass, the gipsy passed close to the Tranter's caravan and as soon as she came parallel to the window, Molly appeared and beckoned her closer.

"Thanks for the needle Shee," she called, opening the latch just a fraction.

Sheila flinched, she hated her name being shortened, "No problem Molly, did it work?"

Molly Tranter stuck up her index finger which was purple and swollen, "I think so."

"Ooh, that looks sore," the psychic commented, "How on earth did you do that?"

"Oh, er, just an accident, anyway must dash," and with that the other woman banged the window shut.

Despite having a busy afternoon with six full readings within three hours, Sheila now and again let her mind wander to the family living across the way. She didn't know Don and Molly Tranter well enough to ask them outright about the visit from the education authority but somehow it seemed like a problem that wasn't going to be resolved overnight and she was determined to find out more.

Therefore, just before seven, having rapidly changed out of her Romany costume and into a pair of jeans and purple sweater, Sheila made a short detour on her way to the Big Top.

"I'll have one please," she told Molly Tranter, who was busy spinning sugar at her candy floss machine, "I fancy a change from ice-cream tonight."

"First time for everything," the vendor commented, carefully inserting a long stick into the sugary web and creating a large ball of pink floss.

Sheila noted the bandage on Molly's index finger and waited for the woman to finish creating the sweet treat, "Haven't had candy floss since I was a young girl, so I haven't."

"Gosh, that long!" Molly tutted, and then realising how rude she must have sounded added, "Sorry Shee, I didn't mean......That sounded awful....I mean...."

The psychic laughed, "I know what you mean, and it WAS a long time ago."

Suddenly the ice was broken between the two women and any tense atmosphere cleared immediately.

"Are you going in to watch the show?" Molly asked, beginning to relax a little.

"To be sure, I always do," Sheila nodded as she carefully tore at a section of candy floss, "I love watching, never miss a night if I can help it. Don't you ever go in?"

"Well, I'm kind of stuck out here aren't I?" Molly joked, pointing at her stall where bagged floss, toffee apples and lollipops were displayed in abundance, "One of these days I will though."

Sheila hadn't given much thought to Molly Tranter's predicament before and wondered if the woman ever got a night off, perhaps leaving her wares in her husband's capable hands.

"Wouldn't Don take a turn one night?" she asked casually, "You know, let you have a break?"

Molly laughed, a loud raucous noise, signalling that Sheila had just made the most ridiculous suggestion ever, "I can tell you've never been married," she managed eventually, "What a thing to say!"

The following morning just after eight, Sheila was outside pegging some washing on the line when she heard the sound of a car approaching. Turning slowly around, she saw the familiar brown Ford Mondeo that had come to the site the previous day.

"Morning," the education officer called as he got of the car, "Lovely day."

"Yes it is," Sheila replied politely, "You're up and about early."

"You know what they say," Mr. Bassett observed, "The early bird catches the worm."

Sheila narrowed her eyes, interested to find out more, "And which worm would you be after then?"

The man simply touched his finger to his nose and sniffed, "Sorry can't say, good day to you."

From her observation point inside the caravan, Sheila watched Andrew Bassett walking purposely over to the Tranter's place, straightening his tie before knocking on the door. Don opened it almost straight away, dressed only in his old jeans and string vest. Sheila looked on as the men exchanged a few words, Don closed the caravan door and then reopened it a couple of minutes later, allowing the other man to enter.

With her source of entertainment temporarily disrupted, Sheila carried on with her cleaning until Luana Chekov appeared with some clothing repairs, keeping the gipsy chatting for a good half hour. By the time she had said goodbye to her visitor and popped her head back outside to see if anything was stirring, Sheila just caught Andrew Bassett returning to his car.

"Everything alright?" she called in a matter of fact way as the officer unlocked the Mondeo.

"As well as it can be," he replied, giving nothing away.

"That's grand," Sheila told him, "Molly and Don are good parents."

"Parents?" Mr. Bassett repeated, his interest sparked, "I was lead to believe they don't have any children."

Sheila immediately realised that she'd put her size six foot right where it didn't belong and started to backtrack, "Well, did I say parents? No, I didn't mean that, I meant they're good people, so I did."

Always alert and ready to smell a rat, the man walked towards the gipsy with his clipboard, smiling.

"So sorry, I didn't catch your name, Mrs?"

"It's Miss, Miss. Hannigan," she told him, wondering what on earth the Tranter's had been saying to excuse themselves from getting into trouble with the authorities, "And I know nothing."

"And by knowing nothing," Andrew Bassett said slowly, "Do you mean that the Tranter's do or do not have two young boys who should be in school?"

Sheila started backing away into her caravan, "Like I said, I haven't got a clue, now I'll say good day to you."

With that she closed the door to her home and breathed heavily, hoping that the man wouldn't knock. Luckily he didn't but, peeking out through the net curtains, Sheila could see him making notes and looking towards the Big Top where Don Tranter was now tacking up a line of bunting. She bit her lip so hard that it bled and cursed profusely. Damn, what had she started now?

For a couple of days, Sheila avoided the Tranters and kept a close watch on any strange cars coming and going. She was terrified that she'd caused the education officer to be on high alert but was also very concerned about the tales that Don and Molly had so obviously been weaving. By the third day, Sheila could control her anxiety no longer and set off on a mission to clear the air.

"And so there you have it," she told Molly Tranter over a pot of tea and an iced bun, "I think I might have upset the apple cart."

"It's alright," Molly sighed, "We knew they'd catch up with us sooner or later, just hoped it would be later."

"How come he didn't catch sight of the boys?" Sheila urged gently, "Did you hide them?"

"In here," the other woman told her, lifting up a bunk unit with empty storage space underneath, "The boys jumped in here and had to stay quiet until he'd gone. Actually, that's how I hurt my finger, Don accidentally closed the top before I'd got my hand out of the way. Oh Shee, what a mess."

Sheila prickled at the sound of her name being shortened again but felt a pang of guilt at having stirred up a pot of trouble. The Tranter's were obviously traditional in their values and didn't want their boys to have a run of the mill education. Sheila suddenly had a moment of inspiration and confided her idea to Molly.

"Now, I'll have to run it past Roly of course," she concluded as she said goodbye to Molly, "But it shouldn't be a problem. You just leave it to me."

Molly Tranter was grateful but didn't look very optimistic, "Alright, let's see what he says. But we have to do something soon, Mr. Bassett's coming back on Monday and he's bringing his boss."

That afternoon, after having spent some time making up roast beef sandwiches and a flask of fresh leek and potato soup, Sheila trudged across the field to see Roly O'Hare. The gaffer was in a crotchety mood and greeted her with a grunt, until he saw the food on offer which changed his outlook completely.

"Well now, what have we here?" he asked, "Don't stand on ceremony Sheila, sit down."

The psychic moved a pile of newspapers and perched on the end of the bunk, wondering how best to put her proposal to this grouchy bear of a man.

"Are you feeling alright today?" she ventured, taking the lid off the flask, "The soup's warm if you'd like some now, and maybe a sandwich on the side?"

Roly sniffed at the blissful aroma of the fresh soup and nodded gratefully, "It smells wonderful Sheila, but I never had you down as a nursemaid."

"I'm just doing my bit to help my boss," she admitted, "You don't think I'd do this if you weren't the gaffer do you, you miserable old sod?"

Roly laughed heartily, this blunt Irishwoman was a rogue but he was grateful that she cared enough to make sure he was eating properly, "It's not laced with arsenic is it?"

"No, it's not," she said indignantly, "I used rat poison, it's quicker."

Roly chuckled and took the cup of soup that was now being offered, enjoying the flavours as they hit his tongue and then licked his lips in appreciation.

"Why haven't you ever married?" he asked suddenly, taking in Sheila's rounded hips and thick curls, "You'd make a smashing wife if someone were fool enough to have you."

Sheila ignored the question but blushed as she felt the old man's eyes on her, "Eat up your soup."

"I'm not daft," Roly spluttered, a globule of soup rolling down his chin, "What is it that you really want?"

That weekend, in between customers and shows, Sheila Hannigan worked endlessly on her project. First she had to call over Dominic and Damon, as they were an integral part of her plan, but getting the boys to keep still while she measured them was a thankless task.

"Why do we have to dress up?" Dominic whined, "I don't get it."

"You've always wanted to be a part of the circus haven't you?" Sheila asked, pulling her tape measure across the child's shoulders, "Now keep still."

"But why do we have to wear those colours?" Damon whinged, holding up a ream of purple fabric, "This is for girls, we'll look like a right pair of poofters.""

"No you won't," the psychic contradicted, "Now please, let's just get on with this."

On Monday morning, dead on nine o'clock, Andrew Bassett arrived at the circus site with his very prim and proper supervisor in tow. Sheila watched the education officer from her door as he scurried around to open the passenger door for his boss, all the while looking flustered and red-faced.

"Top of the morning," Sheila shouted, exaggerating her already pronounced Irish accent.

"Ah, yes, hello Miss. Mulligan," Mr. Bassett called as he ushered his superior out of the car.

"It's fecking Hannigan," Sheila cursed under her breath, still trying to muster a smile, and then more loudly, "I guess you've come to see the Tranter boys."

Andrew Bassett's ears pricked up at the mention of 'boys' and he immediately started walking closer.

"So there are two boys then?" he asked curiously, "Only the other day you said there weren't…"

"Oh, take no notice of me," Sheila huffed, "I don't know my arse from my elbow most days!"

The senior officer, who wore a pin-striped suit and suede loafers which were most certainly the most unsuitable kind of shoes for tackling a muddy field, wrinkled his nose at the woman's language and tugged at his employee's arm to move away from the cause of his disgust.

Before the men had even reached the Tranter's caravan, the door swung open on its hinges and Don Tranter greeted them with a radiant smile.

"Come in gentlemen," he cheered, "You're very welcome, although Damon and Dominic are just about to start their lessons, so please don't disrupt them for too long."

Andrew Bassett peered inside to where a retired professor sat in between the Tranter children at the table. An assortment of books lay open and the man was pointing at map of Scotland.

"You see this line boys?" he was asking, as he traced his finger along the border, "This is Hadrian's Wall. Now who do you think might have wanted to build a border between Scotland and England, mm?"

On seeing the two strangers enter, the professor lifted his head and peered at them over his gold-rimmed spectacles. He was a heavy-set man, with dark piercing eyes that looked at them like an eagle might survey its prey, causing the officers to feel slightly intimidated.

"I'm sorry gentlemen," he said, in a soft Irish accent as he pushed the map to one side, "Can we help you?"

Less than twenty minutes later, Sheila observed Andrew Bassett and his boss picking their way back over the field to the car. She ran outside and pretended to check on her washing, feeling the edges of a lacy petticoat as the men approached.

"Everything alright then?" she chirped, bursting with curiosity, "Did you see the boys?"

"Yes, they were having a history lesson," the senior officer replied, his voice gruff as though he needed to cough, "Seems there was no need for me to come out after all."

Andrew Bassett blushed and looked down at his clipboard, "I honestly thought..."

"Well, you'd best think how to fill out your report when we get back to the office," the older man barked, "There have been enough hours wasted on this case as it is."

"So you won't be coming back?" the gipsy inquired innocently.

"No," Mr. Bassett told her meekly, "Our business here is concluded Miss. Mulligan."

"It's fecking Hannigan," she blurted and then paused, sticking two fingers up at the retreating figures.

The following weekend, as Sheila sat in her spot at the back of the Big Top tent, enjoying the show and picking at a stick of candy floss, Roly O'Hare struggled up the steps to join her and sat down out of breath.

"You're not supposed to be climbing steps in your condition," Sheila cursed.

"And with a figure like yours, you're not supposed to be eating candy floss," the gaffer laughed.

"It was complimentary, from Molly," she told him, "I can't afford to turn down free food."

"Ah, from Molly eh?" Roly wheezed, "As a thank you I suppose?"

Sheila nodded and picked at another strand of the pink sugar.

"You're a smart woman Sheila Hannigan," the old man told her, "Thinking on your feet like that. I guess it's done us all a favour in a way."

Sheila blushed, as she often did in Roly's company, although sometimes it was out of frustration at his brash and forthright manner.

"Well, you've got time on your hands to give the boys a few lessons when you're up to it haven't you Professor?" she chuckled, "In fact I reckon they'll enjoy it?"

Roly nodded, "It certainly fooled those pair of toffs from the authority didn't it? Maybe I've missed my true vocation in life."

"Yes, perhaps," the gipsy told him, "But in the meantime you've gained an extra couple of clowns. It won't hurt the Tranter boys to earn their keep and you need an extra act with Simone going on maternity leave shortly. Everything always happens for a reason Roly."

The gaffer stood slowly, catching his breath before attempting to descend the stairs, "I guess it does Sheila. Oh, and before I forget?"

"Yes?" she said, looking up and expecting another thank you.

"Here are your glasses back," Roly grunted, assuming his usual gruff manner again, and pulling Sheila's gold-rimmed spectacles out of his pocket, "They don't suit me."

Chapter Ten

Roland O'Hare Junior

Tap tappet tap.

It was seven-thirty in the morning and Sheila Hannigan stood with a packet of cigarettes in her hand, debating whether to give in to temptation. She knew that she wouldn't be able to stop at just one and thankfully the knocking at her door saved her from making an immediate decision, so pulling her bobbly old dressing-gown tighter she opened the door.

"Top o' the morning to you Sheila," Roland Junior beamed.

Sheila peered at him with narrowed eyes as she caught a glimpse of the skinny blonde hiding behind the young ringmaster, "Morning, what are you up to now you rascal?"

Roland looked back towards his own trailer and a look of desperation crossed his face, "Can we come in?"

Sheila flung the door wide and stepped back, allowing the young man to bring his lady friend inside.

"Well? Do you want a coffee?"

"No, we're alright," Roland answered before the blonde could open her mouth, "But we need a favour."

Sheila rubbed her tired eyes and looked the waif-like girl up and down, she couldn't have been more than nineteen and was dressed in a thin, strappy dress that barely covered her backside.

"Go on," she sighed, "What is it?"

"Can Tracy stay here until my Da gets up?" Roland blurted, "You know what he's like and I don't need a lecture. We meant to sneak out earlier but we lost track of time."

Sheila sucked in her breath. She didn't approve of the youngster's womanising but he was a good looking chap and it was only natural to have his fair share of ladies stopping over.

"Alright," she finally agreed, "But as soon as you see him going over to the Big Top you can come and fetch her and take her home."

"Thanks," the girl muttered, a rosy blush rising in her cheeks, "I appreciate it."

"Mmm, well," Sheila chuntered, more to herself than anyone in particular, "Let's make you a warm drink and get you a cardigan to wear, your arse must be freezing in that slip of a dress."

It was another hour before Roly left his caravan and sauntered over to the circus tent to check on preparations for the show. He had a daily ritual of finding something to complain about before then telling Jake Collins and his band of workers what a good job they were doing and this particular day was no different. True to his word though, as soon as he spotted his father up and about, Roland Junior started up his truck and drove it across the grass to Sheila's place.

"You're a star," he grinned, cheekily giving the gipsy a peck on the cheek, "You've saved me a lot of earache so you have."

"Well, just don't make a habit of it," Sheila scolded, "See you Tracy love."

The shy young teenager batted her eyelids and began removing the other woman's woolly cardigan that she'd loaned, "Bye Sheila, nice to meet you."

"Oh, you can keep that," the Irishwoman suddenly decided, "What on earth will your folks think if you turn up half-dressed?"

Tracy shrugged and pulled the purple clothing back over her shoulders, "You're very kind."

"Right, come on," ushered Roland, holding the door open, "Let's get going."

It wasn't until after lunch that Sheila saw the young ringmaster again and by that time she'd changed into her traditional fortune-telling attire and was setting up ready for the first reading.

"Uh-hum," Roland coughed, "Can I come in?"

Sheila turned swiftly around, coming face to face with a bouquet of fragrant flowers.

"Oh my word," she gasped, "Are those for me?"

"Well I don't see anyone else in here……" Roland began, rolling his eyes around the room playfully.

"You didn't need to do that…" the gipsy enthused.

"Well, it's not only a thank you for this morning," the handsome man told her, "But a token of my appreciation for everything you've been doing for my Da. Although you did save me today."

"Will you being seeing Tracy again?" Sheila asked, but as soon as the words left her mouth she knew the answer. Roland was a player, just like his father had been in his youth and a young woman like Tracy had no permanent place in his life.

"I'm not the settling type Sheila," he explained, "Besides, girls who go around wearing next to nothing and caked in make-up really aren't my idea of marriage material."

"But you're twenty-eight," the psychic tutted, "Do you not want a family of your own?"

"Ask me in two years," he grinned, ducking out through the door, "Look, your first customer's here."

Working her way through half a dozen clients that afternoon, Sheila was struck by how their expectations were all very similar and not too far removed from her own life goals. All six readings were for middle-aged ladies, five of them married and one spinster. Despite being in permanent relationships, the married women still expected to hear news that something fun and exciting was about to enter their lives, sadly 'Psychic Sheila' was unable to comply with their wishes. Peering down into her crystal ball and mustering up images, she didn't see any Premium Bond winners or long-lost millionaire relatives bestowing money upon her customers, no, instead she saw quite mundane lives with the odd family holiday and a few house moves. As for the spinster, she could see an inheritance, but it also foretold of a loss, as the lady in question lived with her elderly parents and the property was coming to her as a direct result of their death. No matter how the fortune-teller tried to dress it up, there weren't glamorous lifestyles awaiting these housewives, just years of housework and keeping their heads above water.

"Well, nothing out of the ordinary Mrs. Livingstone," she told her last paying customer, "Although I can see a trip to far off shores next year, somewhere hot and sunny."

"Oh, lovely," the woman smiled, "My Steven said he might book us a family holiday to Spain."

"Well it looks like he'll be true to his word then," Sheila grinned, "Hope you have a lovely time."

The woman opened her purse and took out a crisp new note with which to pay for Sheila's services, pausing to ask a question before she left, "Do you see your own future? I mean, do you always know what's going to happen, or does it only work for other people?"

Sheila sighed and decided to tell the truth, after all she might never see this particular client again, "I see everything and sometimes I really don't like what I see, but it's the knowledge that something good is going to happen to me sooner or later that keeps me going."

That evening, as she entered the Big Top, Sheila caught a glimpse of Roland O'Hare waiting in the wings. She couldn't resist the urge to check up on him and sneaked under the canvas flap to say hello. As for Roland O'Hare, he didn't hear the gipsy sneaking up behind him and was caught unawares. The ringmaster had his hand down the back of his tight jodhpurs and was wriggling uncomfortably.

"What the hell's the matter?" Sheila whispered, "Have you gone and caught something nasty?"

Roland jumped at the sound of her voice and removed his hand from the trousers.

"Jeez," he cursed, "Are you spying on me?"

"No, I am fecking not," Sheila swore, "I came to wish you luck with the show, how was I to know you'd be playing with yourself?"

"I am not…" Roland began through gritted teeth, "I've got an itch, so I have."

"So I see," the gipsy cackled before walking away, "I'll leave you to it."

Looking down from her elevated position on the back tier of the audience, Sheila had a great view of the performers, including their flamboyant ringmaster, although she did need to put on her glasses to see the show properly and now sat with the gold-rimmed spectacles perched precariously on her nose. She felt slightly guilty that she'd teased 'The Great Rolando' before his big entrance and could still see a trace of annoyance on the young man's face as he walked around the ring with arms akimbo announcing the next act. As the crowd clapped and cheered enthusiastically, pride swelled up in Sheila's chest for her fellow circus family members and at that moment in time she had no reservations whatsoever about a life on the road. Perhaps she did feel over-protective towards the younger members of the group, especially towards young Roland, but that was only natural for a woman of her age, wasn't it?

As Sheila cast her eyes over the lithe figure of Luana Chekov now balancing on a tightrope, then across to where Sergei waited with baited breath, the gipsy took in the sounds of the audience's appreciation. She could see Ray Stubbs's heavy iron weights next to the huge red curtain and knew instinctively that he'd be performing in a few moments, but as Luana somersaulted her way to the ground to a roaring crowd, 'The Great Rolando' failed to enter the ring to announce the next act. Taking their cue from the bandmaster, who quickly instructed his musicians to strike up a tune, the Chekovs flick-flacked around the inner part of the circle, to a standing ovation while Ray quickly hunted for the ringmaster.

Just before the end of 'Nelly the Elephant', played with a lead part for the trombone, aimed at the children in the audience, 'The Great Rolando' bounced into the ring, looking flustered and flushed. Sheila leaned forward to get a closer look but couldn't find a hint of why the young man looked so hot and bothered. She sincerely hoped he hadn't been canoodling with a young lady during his ten minutes off stage. Maybe she needed a quiet word in his ear.

After the evening show, Sheila sat patiently in her seat waiting for the crowd to disperse. Most people were making their way towards the outdoor arena where Danger McDougall was scheduled to ride his motorbike over a line of battered old cars especially provided for this venue by a local breaker's yard. Sheila had been looking forward to this particular event all day but, weighing up her moral responsibilities, decided to seek out Roland O'Hare to find out what on earth was going on. It didn't take long to locate the ringmaster in his trailer, although Sheila could have timed her visit better and saved herself a great deal of embarrassment.

Rock music was playing quite loudly inside young Roland's mobile home and despite Sheila Hannigan knocking several times the occupant didn't hear her so, never being one to stand on ceremony, she opened the door and let herself in. Unfortunately, what Sheila received at that precise moment was not a warm greeting, but an eyeful of the ringmaster's very red and sore bottom.

"Oh Hell," she screeched, covering her eyes, "I'm so sorry, I did knock."

"What the…?" a very alarmed Roland yelled, struggling to pull on his jeans, "Christ Sheila, what are you doing in here woman?"

Pulling herself together rapidly despite the shock, Sheila looked him square in the eye and the asked the obvious question, "What on earth is the matter with your backside, it's as red as a tomato?"

"Ay well, that's none of your concern," Roland said sharply, "Now if you don't mind giving a man a bit of privacy…"

"Come on," Sheila soothed, not moving an inch, "Maybe I can help."

Roland suddenly resigned himself to the fact that the woman wasn't going to leave and relented slightly, "I honestly have no idea, except that it's as sore as hell and it really is driving me mad."

"Well, drop your trousers," Sheila sighed, "I can't help without having a proper look."

Back in her caravan, Sheila emptied out the medicine cabinet to see if she had a suitable lotion to treat Roland's skin. It was a strange one, she thought, something between nappy rash and scarletina but she was sure that some soothing calamine lotion would do the trick. The problem was, due to the location of the redness, the ringmaster was going to need some help to apply it.

"You're going to have to come over morning and night to let me put it on for you," Sheila explained, "Unless you've got some woman over there that can do it for you."

"Bloody hell," Roland cursed, "That's all I need, Sheila Hannigan bum doctor extraordinaire!"

"Well, it's either that or ask your Da," Sheila chuckled, "And somehow I don't think that's an option."

"No, it's not," he conceded, "This is unbelievable."

"And you've no idea how you got it Roland?"

"Not a clue," he relented, shaking his head and bending over, "Come on Sheila, get it over with."

A week or so later, having seen to it that her patient's rash was completely clear and that he no longer needed to come over for twice daily treatment, Sheila was packing up her belongings ready for the next move. The following morning they would be driving East in convoy, to the part of England where the land was flat and canal boats drifted along waterways in the countryside. Sheila loved these kind of locations, especially watching the scenery go by as she reclined on her bunk and was looking forward to staying in a more tranquil spot than usual away from the bustling towns. Just as she popped the last of her china ornaments into a box, a familiar face appeared at the window.

"I've got something for you," Roland O'Hare called, holding up Sheila's old purple cardigan, "That bird brought it back this afternoon."

"That bird?" Sheila echoed, opening the window and taking the knitted jacket, "Do you mean Tracy?"

"Yes, that's it," the cheeky young man laughed, "Never was very good at remembering names."

"You should be ashamed of yourself," Sheila scolded, "She was quite a pretty young thing."

Roland shrugged, there was a twinkle in his eye as if he was waiting for something, but Sheila shut the window before she said something that she might later regret.

That afternoon, with a couple of hours free and no bookings, Sheila decided to make the most of the warm sunshine with a brisk walk in the countryside. She knew that by walking just half an hour or so to the south of the camping ground, there was a small riverside tavern that served good food. She'd been there a few years previously with some of the group but today she sought solitude and tranquillity, whether she found it or not was a different matter completely.

Picking up her purple cardigan from the bottom of the bunk where she'd left it that morning, the psychic sniffed at it and then cursed. It had a stale perfume smell mixed with sweat. Sheila wrinkled up her nose and took the item outside where she promptly deposited it in dustbin.

"Damn that Roland and his women," Sheila muttered, going back inside to find another sweater to take with her on the walk, "I'll never understand him as long as I live."

When she stepped outside again, Jake Collins was there, looking sheepish.

"I've got a couple of hours free," he blurted, "Look I know you don't approve of what I did, but at least let me try to explain will you?"

Sheila sighed and forced a smile, "Look Jake love, it's up to you how you live your life, and it's certainly none of my business. I'm off for a stroll, you can come if you like."

The tent master grinned. It had been several weeks since Sheila had spoken to him properly, in fact she'd been cold towards him since she had discovered his secret, but he dearly hoped that they could reconcile their friendship and perhaps even spark a touch of romance.

"I'll treat you to lunch," he offered, "And this time we'll have a proper meal."

"Hold on," a deep voice called from behind them, "Are you going for something to eat?"

The pair turned and saw Ray Stubbs striding towards them, waving his right arm.

Sheila greeted him warmly and slipped one arm through Ray's and the other through Jake's.

"The more the merrier," she chuckled, trying to ignore the sharp glare that Jake was giving her, "Now then shall we go? I could murder a steak and onion pie."

"You're sure I'm not going to be gooseberry?" Ray whispered to his friend.

Sheila nudged him and cackled, "No, Raymond, I think you might have just saved the day."

It was pleasantly warm with a slight breeze, but Sheila felt the additional warmth of her two strong companions as they walked along arm in arm admiring the scenery and making general conversation. She could sense that Jake was a bit dejected but tried her best to lift his mood by telling tales of the customers she'd had in her caravan that week.

"Well, Daisy Jacobs," she explained as they neared the river, "She's eighty-three and was asking me if she'd find love again, have you ever heard the like? Bless her."

The men laughed heartily as they listened to Sheila doing a bad impression of the old woman's Cockney accent, something which she enjoyed much more than she would ever let on.

"Here we are," Ray announced, as the trio reached the beer garden of the tavern, "You two find a table and I'll fetch the drinks, what are you having?"

It was fairly busy for a weekday afternoon, with a vast number of white collar workers having escaped their stuffy offices for a lunch break, but there was one table free at the edge of the grass. Within minutes Ray was back with their order and he was smiling ear to ear.

"You'll never guess who's in there?" he boomed, "Young Roland, with a bit of crumpet."

"Crumpets?" Sheila echoed, "At lunchtime? That'll never keep him going."

Jake gave her a playful wink and explained, "Not crumpets Sheila, you daft mare, totty, floosy, a young woman, a bit of stuff."

Sheila's mouth formed an 'O' and before her friend could say any more she set off inside.

"Do you reckon she's soft on Roland?" Ray asked, taking a sip of his beer,

"Dunno," Jake replied, "But she didn't hang about did she? Roland wouldn't be interested in Sheila would he? I mean, there must be nearly twenty years between them."

"He seems to chase after anything in a skirt," muttered the strongman, "Why not Sheila?"

Jake conceded that although the scenario were unlikely, it wasn't impossible, "Maybe something has already happened between them and she's gone in there to confront him."

Ray looked down at his pint and sighed, "I hope not, I've quite taken a shine to Sheila, and by the looks of things you have too Jake. May the best man win."

Inside the pub, Sheila had managed to control her initial instincts to give Roland a piece of her mind and, pretending to need the toilet, had brushed past him in an accidental manner.

"Oh, I'm so sorry," she smiled apologetically, "I didn't see you there. How are you?"

"Who's this, your mother?" the dark-haired woman at Roland's side sniffed, looking Sheila up and down.

"Hey, now this happens to be a very good friend of mine," the ringmaster interjected, "Be nice."

Sheila had seen and heard enough to know that the young woman wasn't a well-mannered person and she stood appraising her clothing, or the lack of it. Dressed in a very short denim skirt and a low-cut top, there was little left to the imagination, putting the girl ever lower down in the psychic's estimation.

"I'll see you later," Sheila Hannigan tutted, heading for the lavatory, "And for Christ's sake be careful."

There was tittering from the young woman as Sheila headed down the corridor and a frown furrowed her brow as she contemplated Roland's choice of drinking partner. She sincerely hoped that this one wouldn't have to be sneaked off the camp tomorrow morning.

Putting her thoughts and concerns about Roland temporarily aside, Sheila enjoyed a hearty lunch with her two friends. It was obvious that the pair had been talking about her behind her back and the gipsy instinctively felt that there was a degree of competition between the two men.

"Aren't you going to eat your peas?" she teased Ray, knowing full well that he didn't like greens.

And then, "You've spilled gravy on your shirt Jake, you mucky pup."

The men took Sheila's mothering in good humour and vied for her attention like teenagers. By the time they had to set off back to the site, both Ray and Jake were like putty in her hands. Lunch had been good fun, it certainly wasn't often that the psychic commanded the attention of two handsome men but today she could be bothered to favour neither. Consuming her thoughts on the walk home was Roland O'Hare and nobody else. She wasn't jealous of the young man's womanising but it did rub her up the wrong way. If he happened to get a girl pregnant, Sheila knew that it would be her that Roland would turn to. After all, with his mother gone and Roly being so ill, there wouldn't be anyone else whom he could trust to sort out such a pickle. She wondered whether she should give the man a lecture on contraception, although being an Irish Catholic it might well fall on deaf ears but the least she could do was try.

The opportunity to lecture Roland O'Hare about his immoral antics didn't arrive until the following morning when, enjoying her coffee on the doorstep as usual, Sheila spied him sneaking a red-haired woman out of his trailer. The young lady's skin was as white as snow but the unmistakable hue of a freckled complexion was clearly evident. Sheila watched as Roland ushered the girl into his truck and told her to keep her head down as

160

he drove out onto the main road. At that point Sheila rushed to get dressed. She wanted to be waiting when the rampant young man returned.

Less than fifteen minutes had passed when Roland returned, and Sheila was still trying desperately to untangle her hair with a huge paddle brush, cursing and swearing as she tugged at her unruly mop. However, on hearing the truck drive past her window, Sheila flung open the door and marched across to the young ringmaster's trailer. Unbeknown to the psychic, both Jake and Ray had spotted her from their respective vantage points around the circus ground.

"Get inside," Sheila tutted at Roland as he jumped out of the vehicle, "I need a word."

"Whoa there," the young man chortled, "Where's the fire?"

"In your underpants I should think," Sheila scoffed, wagging her finger crossly, "You can make me a coffee while you explain what you've been up to. If your father knew he'd have your guts for garters."

Roland opened the door and allowed the irate woman to enter first, he hadn't been spoken to in this way since his mother had been alive and it amused him immensely.

"Right," he sighed, having filled the kettle and sat down opposite Sheila at the table, "Out with it."

For ten minutes, Sheila let fire with a tirade of lecturing on the merits of having good moral standards, how contraception was the key to modern living despite their religious upbringing and how young women nowadays were too loose in their outlook.

She finished with a reference to Tammy O'Hare saying, "Your poor Mammy would turn in her grave if she knew what you were up to every night."

Finally Roland spoke, keeping his eyes fixed on Sheila the whole time, "Are you jealous?"

"Don't be ridiculous," the gipsy spluttered, putting her hand to her breast, "I'm trying to look out for you, because I care about you, as a, a friend, and no more, can't you see?"

The young man flexed his muscles and silently got up to make his guest a hot drink and a couple of minutes passed in silence before he spoke again.

"Sheila," he began, rubbing a hand through his hair, "I don't know how to tell you this, in fact it's really embarrassing, so it is, but I haven't had sex with any of those girls."

Sheila coughed, spluttering coffee over the table, "If you expect me to believe that, you're a fool Roland O'Hare, I've seen the way you are."

"And how am I?" he replied softly, getting up for a cloth to wipe the coffee stains.

"All flirty," Sheila carried on, "And having women back here night after night."

The ringmaster sighed and pulled a thick black folder out from under the sink. Silently he opened it and showed Sheila what was inside.

Page after page held beautiful photographs of women in circus costumes. The outfits were obviously vintage and must have cost a packet but the way that the girls were dressed and made up was exquisite, only a professional could have created such amazing artwork.

"What are these?" Sheila whispered as she gently turned the pages in awe.

"My hobby," Roland confessed, "I'm making an album of circus memorabilia to sell in aid of the heart foundation. It will be in my Da's memory."

A tightening sensation crept up into Sheila's throat as she fought back a tear, "Are you telling me the truth? You mean you haven't been taking advantage of those girls?"

Roland shook his head and then crossed his chest, "I swear Sheila. Sometimes it takes hours to get the pictures right and so it's morning by the time we finish, I'm fair knackered so I am."

The psychic sat thinking as she stopped at a particularly stylish photo where the young model was posing with a lion tamer's whip in her hand, "But all this stuff, where did it come from?"

"Been in the family for decades," he answered, "Rolando's is a fifth generation circus you know, our ancestors go back to before Queen Victoria's day."

"I had no idea," Sheila smiled, "Just imagine how proud your Da's going to be when you tell him, he'll be over the moon, I can hardly believe you're a secret photographer, it's amazing."

Roland took the binder and slipped it back into its hiding place, "Best keep it out of sight for now."

Sheila nodded but then had a moment of revelation, "Wait a minute!" she sneered, "What about that awful red rash all over your backside?"

The young man flushed, deciding whether to come clean with the rest of the story.

"It's from the nylon," he confessed, "I wear ladies knickers when I'm in the ring. You see my jodhpurs are so tight that you can see every outline of regular bloke's underwear, so I buy a small size of women's pants to wear underneath."

Sheila suppressed a laugh, "So the knickers, they don't belong to the girls?"

"No! No way!" Roland gasped, "I'm not a pervert!"

"Thank the Lord for that, I think I've heard about as much as I can take for one day."

"Sheila," Roland said as she got up to leave, "I've only got eyes for one woman, you should know that."

She closed the door behind her without looking back.

Sitting with her cocoa and 'The Royal Variety Performance' on television later that night, Sheila replayed the earlier conversation with Roland in her mind. She believed every word he'd told her, it was simply too bizarre not to, besides her psychic intuition had told her that the young man was telling the truth and that counted for a lot. But what about that last confession? Did he mean what she thought he did? It really was too crazy to contemplate. Maybe she should try to put some distance between herself and Roland, for everyone's sake, although deep in her heart Sheila knew that a request of that sort was totally unreasonable. She yearned to sit down and have a heart to heart with the youngster, although coming up to twenty-nine next birthday, he was a fully grown man and therefore apt to know his own mind.

Sheila sipped at the thick milky chocolate, now going cold, and turned her thoughts towards the man's father. There had been times in the past twelve months when the old man had warned Sheila against getting too close to his son, but very soon all that would change. Once Roly O'Hare was gone, Sheila would be free to do as she liked, no matter what anyone said.

Chapter Eleven

Gipsy Rose

Roly O'Hare cleared his throat and looked at the group of faces staring blankly back at him.

"It's time for us to take a break," he announced gruffly, stuffing his calloused hands deep into his trouser pockets, "So, you can follow to us to Ireland and take what work I can find for you during the Winter months or you can return to your families and enjoy a Christmas together. Let me know what you decide by the end of the day and I'll start making arrangements to leave."

"What kind of work will there be?" Danger McDougall asked, "Simone won't be able to work after the New Year so I'll need to support her and the baby."

"Don't you worry," Roly replied, his mood mellowing somewhat, "I've got plenty of connections in the business and I know for sure that a man of your talents would be able to get a season contract with 'Hannigan's Circus' in Dublin?"

The stuntman immediately clicked on at the name and turned to Sheila behind him, "Any relation?"

"Don't be daft," she whispered, feeling slightly uncomfortable, "If it was I wouldn't be here working for that grumpy old git."

They both turned their attention back to Roly who was gesturing to his son, "Roland here will make a note of what you all decide, and those who aren't coming with us should leave contact details for the Spring."

"What are you doing?" Ray Stubbs asked Sheila as they left the circus tent, "I'm going back to spend time with my mum, you could come with me if you like?"

"Wouldn't that mean living under the same roof?" Sheila joked, "No, I think I'll go back to the old country and look up some friends. We'll be back together again soon enough Raymond."

The strongman liked that she referred to him by his full name and gave his friend a quick hug, "Don't you go finding yourself another fella Sheila Hannigan, I'll still be waiting when you come back."

The woman blushed and shook her head, "There's about as much chance of that as a plague of locusts."

"Well, if you change your mind, you know where I am," Ray told her, "I've written down the phone number for you, you know, just in case," and handing her a slip of paper, the man walked away.

"Are you coming with us darling?" Roland asked, tapping Sheila on the shoulder as she stood thinking.

"Well, I have nowhere else to be," she sighed, "Besides, it might be time to put a few demons to rest."

The young man gave her an inquisitive look but that was all Sheila was prepared to say on the matter.

"I'll get packed up," she said instead, "I take it we're leaving at dawn?"

The journey was a rough one. Firstly a two hundred mile road-trip up to the ferry port on the other side of the country and then a stormy boat ride across the Irish Sea. Sheila was fine riding along in the back of her caravan but, as soon as they set sail, she felt as though her stomach were churning around inside a washing-machine. The waves lashed up the side of the boat and every time the sea-sick passengers went outside for a breath of fresh air, they came back even greener than before. Roly and his son were unaffected by the tides and spent most of the passage propping up the bar. Simone was fine too, sipping hot tea and reading a crime novel while Danger McDougall stayed within easy reach of the nearest toilet. Although not physically sick, Sheila fought to keep control of her urge to release the fried breakfast she'd rather foolishly eaten that morning and sat breathing through her nose until the ferry arrived in port.

The air was fresh and the land green. Sheila had missed her home country and took in the sights around her as the convoy moved off the boat and on to dry land. It had been ten years since she'd set foot upon Irish soil and the feeling of homesickness finally removed itself as she surveyed the beautiful scenery.

"Do you have family nearby?" Simone asked gently, seeing the pain in Sheila's eyes.

"Not far away," the gipsy whispered, "Not far away at all."

Simone sensed that there was more than met the eye but she wasn't about to push her friend into a confession, so moved swiftly away to where her lover was starting up the truck.

"Ride in the front with me," Roland urged, taking Sheila by the shoulder, "You'll see things better from the cab, and besides, I need to know where to drop you off."

"Oh, I'll just come to the caravan site with you for now," Sheila responded, "That's if it's alright. I don't have anywhere I need to be in a hurry and I'd much rather sleep in my own home anyway. There will be plenty of time for reunions later."

For the first week of her time in Dublin, Sheila carried on as usual, just without her customers. She baked cakes and biscuits for Roly O'Hare, took walks around the town window-shopping and spent the evenings watching television in her caravan. She wasn't exactly lonely but Sheila needed time to think. How could she just turn up at her family home without a word?

As the years had passed, it had become harder and harder to sit down and write a letter, besides she hardly knew what to say anymore. Events from the past had caused a rift between Sheila and her family, and turning up on the doorstep now would certainly be no easy task.

By the second week, Sheila Hannigan was beginning to feel a little more like her old brave self and decided to take the bus to the housing estate where her aunt lived. Her strategy was to test the water and decide what to do after that.

Diana O' Connell was Sheila's maternal aunt and bore a striking resemblance to her own mother despite the two women being five years apart in age. She bore no malice towards her niece and ushered Sheila into a room she referred to as the parlour, bringing out the best china teacups and slices of fruit cake.

"Sorry I don't have much to offer," Diana explained, "It's hard trying to live on just a pension, things are so expensive these days so they are."

Sheila nodded and looked around the room at the family photographs. She recognised her mother in her teenage years, in a white gown when she had married Patrick Hannigan at just twenty-one and in a later group photo surrounded by grown-up children.

"Thanks Aunty Di," she said as the tea was poured, "It seems strange being back here."

"Well, what I want to know," Diana began, smoothing down her skirt and sitting in an armchair, "Is why you've come back now? And have you been over to see your Da yet?"

Sheila shook her head, "Not yet, I don't know what to say to him."

"Well, you could try explaining where you've been for the past decade," Diana chided her, but then seeing her niece's face, she softened and rubbed the woman's hand, "Look I know it'll be hard making contact again but I know for a fact that he misses you."

"Really?" Sheila asked, unconvinced that her father would forgive her for leaving, "He told me it was my duty to look after him and the boys when Ma died. He wanted me to stay there like some unpaid slave, and with everything that went on before, well, I just couldn't."

"Well, I have an idea," said Diana O'Connell in a low voice so as not to wake her husband who was napping in the next room, "Come round for your tea tomorrow and I'll have everything ready for you."

Sheila listened as her aunt explained the plan, wondering if they could really pull it off but also confident that she had nothing to lose if it all backfired.

"Alright," she said finally, picking up her handbag, "I'll see you tomorrow Aunty Di."

The following evening, after sharing a hearty stew with her aunt and uncle, Sheila boarded the late night bus back to the campsite with a bag of clothes tucked under her arm. First thing the next morning she planned to call on Roly O' Hare as she, Sheila Hannigan, was in need of a new job.

Three days later, Roland Junior drove the psychic across town to her first job interview in a decade. Sheila was naturally nervous and fidgeted non-stop as the truck rolled along, but she was also feeling rather strange dressed up in the clothes that her Aunt Diana had provided her with, especially the long black wig which was made of nylon and made her head itch constantly.

"Why are you in disguise?" Roland asked, smirking at Sheila as she tucked a stray strand of her own hair under the headscarf, "Are you trying to make yourself look younger?"

"No, I just want to look different, that's all," she snapped, "Different clientele, different look."

They pulled up and the young man watched Sheila get out of the vehicle, "I'll be back for you in an hour, and make sure you tell them it's only temporary, we need you back after Christmas."

Sheila waved Roland away and stood staring at the huge banner displaying the logo of 'Hannigan's Circus.' It hadn't changed since her youth but the lettering had faded to pastel shades from being outside in all weather, a sign of the thrifty way in which Patrick Hannigan always conducted his business. She took a few steps forward and listened to the sounds of the circus folk at work, the band practising, ponies trotting around the ring inside the tent and the unmistakable hammering of men at work. The smells were the same as those at 'Rolando's', the sweetness of the candy floss machine being warmed up, smoke from a wood fire inside one of the caravans and cherry tobacco from a pipe being smoked by the circus owner. The former smell being strong and lingering as Sheila caught sight of Patrick Hannigan walking towards her, a recognition that told her that despite his greying hair, her father hadn't changed a bit.

"Rose?" the man called as he crossed the grass towards Sheila, "Are you Rose Heggarty?"

"That I am," lied Sheila, conjuring up a fake smile, "Also known as Gipsy Rose."

"Come on over to my trailer," the man gestured, pointing towards a shabby caravan, "I'll make some tea."

Sheila followed her father as he sauntered across the field. He was still as stocky and dark as she remembered but he'd lost some of his hair on the crown, and a bald spot invaded his thick curls. She felt as chill run down her spine as she recalled his violent temper, never physical but enough to put the fear of God into Sheila and her siblings.

"Here we are," Patrick announced, opening the door, "Sit yourself down girl."

Everything inside the man's home looked dated. It was as though time had stood still for Patrick Hannigan since his wife had passed away and even the tea towel on the draining board had lost its once vibrant print. Sheila recognised it as her mother's favourite, one she'd picked out on a family trip to Cork when the children were young, it should have been thrown out a long time ago.

"So, Rose," Mr. Hannigan coughed, stirring Sheila from her thoughts, "I reckon the best way for me to test your ability is to have you read the tea leaves in my cup. You don't have a problem with that do you?"

Sheila flicked her eyes back to the speaker, realising that she was being spoken to, "Well, I usually like to use a crystal ball, but I'm sure that tea leaves will suffice for today's purposes."

Patrick poured a cup for each of them as he studied the woman before him and drank the hot liquid. She looked familiar, he thought, although it was hard to tell properly with all the heavy make-up she was wearing, perhaps he'd seen her at one of the other showgrounds on his travels.

"Have you ever been to Tipperary?" he asked, trying to figure out where he might have seen Gipsy Rose.

Sheila shook her head, causing the nylon wig to tickle the back of her neck again, "No, never."

Patrick took a last gulp of his tea and handed the cup over to have his fortune told. He was sceptical about the abilities of women who claimed to have a sixth sense in these matters but his own wife had been the seventh child of a seventh child and she had certainly had the knack for foreseeing the future. It had made him a pot of gold too, if he was honest, and he missed her dearly both for her home-cooking and for the regular cash that she'd added to their growing fortune.

"You lost someone very dear to you about ten years ago," Gipsy Rose told the circus owner, "Was it your wife perhaps?"

Patrick Hannigan raised an eyebrow but gave nothing away, "Go on."

"You have seven children," she mumbled slowly, pretending to focus on the leaves in the bottom of the cup, "And you're close to all of them except the girl, who is the youngest."

Sheila kept a watchful eye on the reaction of her father as she pondered what to reveal next, she didn't want to push him too far, but then again she didn't want to let him off lightly either.

"Well, if you know so much," Patrick ventured, trying to keep his voice steady despite the growing unease, "Where is she now? Can you tell me that?"

"Sorry," Gipsy Rose simpered, putting down the china cup, "I can't see that, the shapes are unclear."

Patrick studied the woman's face as she bent over the cup and tried to weigh her up. He liked her, there was an uncanny likeness to his late wife who, incidentally had also been called Rose.

There was an uncomfortable silence as Gipsy Rose waited for Mr. Hannigan speak again, "So you're looking for work to tide you over until the spring?

"That's right," Sheila told him, careful not to look her father in the eye, "I'll be on my way on March 1st."

"Right, that'll do fine, so it will," Patrick told her, "Welcome to Hannigan's Circus Gipsy Rose."

Sheila sat in silence on the journey back to the caravan park, despite Roland urging her to tell him all about her interview. She didn't know whether she'd done the right thing by getting involved with her father's circus, but Sheila desperately wanted to see how her brothers were faring. Seeing her father had stirred up a lot of old memories, some of them good but a few negative ones too, things that had been safely locked away in the closets of her mind for a long, long time.

"Why don't I take you out to celebrate your new job?" Roland was asking, a smile playing on his lips.

"What about your Da?" Sheila replied, "You shouldn't leave him on his own for too long."

"He'll be alright," the young man told her, "He can barely stay awake after eight o'clock these days."

"I'll come over and cook for you," Sheila decided, the last thing she needed was to be alone with Roland at the moment, "I'll just go and get out of these ridiculous clothes. Now, you go and fetch a bottle of wine."

Two months passed and Sheila, or Gipsy Rose, as she was now calling herself, fell into a routine in her new position as resident fortune-teller at Hannigan's Circus. Patrick had rigged up a purple and gold tent for during her working hours, so Sheila returned to her caravan on the campsite every night. In fact, Roland O'Hare had insisted upon driving her to and fro to her new job, easing the journey considerably. Roly O'Hare also spent a good deal of time at the circus ground. As it happened, he had been business partners with Patrick Hannigan some years ago and enjoyed catching up on the man's business progress in what he termed 'the old country'. There were many days when Sheila would see the silhouettes of the two men sitting in the warmth of her father's trailer, laughing and drinking as they reminisced.

It wasn't hard for Sheila to fool her father into thinking that she was an outsider. For a start, the disguise had helped, but in truth Sheila had been a much slimmer woman when she left Ireland and the pounds had left her with a different figure and fuller face. Although she was desperate to see her brothers, Sheila couldn't risk her father finding out who she was and therefore had to content herself with watching the boys from afar. Dermot and Daniel, the twins, had become accomplished horse riders and made their living dazzling the crowds with their bareback skills. Eamon was chief rigger and took control of any maintenance that needed doing around the place and Sheila had often bumped into Sean and Steven as they toiled away under their brother's watchful eye. Patrick Junior, the eldest, helped his father to control the purse strings and was a self-taught accountant, nothing got past him proving that he was most definitely his father's son both in name and nature.

Sheila didn't know if she would ever reveal herself to Patrick Hannigan. She remembered the way in which he had treated her as a teenager, threatening her with his leather belt and shouting a torrent of abuse. He had never actually laid a hand upon her, or the boys for that matter, but they were all scared that one day he might just take his frustration out on them and leave physical scars as well as mental ones. Her mother's death had been the escape route that Sheila had waited for, and if it hadn't been for that she might have waited another decade or more before finally breaking her family ties. A cloud had always hung over her head due to what Patrick Hannigan had referred to as 'the incident' and not a day went by that Sheila didn't think about and the consequences it had had on her adult life. For now she was just happy to observe her brothers, seeing that they had grown into strong and handsome men was a godsend but the heartache was raw as she forced herself to stay anonymous.

The fortune-telling part of her disguise was a piece of cake for Sheila Hannigan. Having spent her whole life with the ability to read people and connect with their lives, reading Tarot cards and tea-leaves wasn't too difficult. The customers in Ireland didn't pay as well as those in England, but she made enough.

As Christmas drew near, Roly O'Hare became weaker. He found it hard to walk due to his breathing difficulties and had lost his appetite, despite Sheila's best efforts at baking his favourite treats. Young Roland did his best to keep the old man's spirits up but it had become evident that his father needed more care than either he or Sheila could give him.

"I think it might be time for Da to go into a nursing home," Roland confessed to Sheila on their ride to the circus one frosty December morning, "I don't think he's got much time left."

His companion blinked and decided how best to answer, "I think you might be right."

"Really? Thank goodness you agree," the man sighed, "I thought you might think I was being harsh."

"Well," Sheila conceded, "He's in need of round the clock care and you simply can't give it. You can't keep your eye on him twenty-four hours a day and with me working it's impossible for us to take shifts. Do you have somewhere in mind?"

Roland nodded, "There's a place not far away, for terminally ill patients. It'll be costly though, not that I mind but I'm not exactly a rich man."

"Talk to your Da," she replied softly, placing a hand on Roland's arm, "He might have some money put aside for a rainy day."

"Trust me Sheila, I know how much he's got and it's not a fortune."

Sheila's eyes twinkled as she pressed her fingers into his shirt sleeves, "Ask him. You might be surprised. But make sure you tell him it's only because you care about him."

That evening, when he picked her up from the circus, Roland had news for Sheila.

"There's no way will Da go into a care home," the young man confessed, "He went up like a bottle of pop when I suggested it, says he'd rather have you looking after him."

"Me?" Sheila shrieked, her eyes wide and startled, "Why the hell would he want me?"

"He says he trusts you," Roland explained, slowing down the truck, "Would you at least think about it?"

Sheila took a handkerchief out and dabbed her hot brow, "I don't suppose I have a choice do I?"

That night Sheila Hannigan didn't sleep a wink. Taking care of Roly would mean that she would have to bring her plans forward with immediate effect and she wasn't entirely sure if she was ready. The previous week's spent working at Hannigan's Circus weren't about the money, although it did come in handy, as Sheila had saved more than enough to see her through until 'Rolando's Circus' was back on the road again. She also knew that Roly O'Hare wouldn't be coming with them. This trip to Ireland was his last chance to say goodbye to the few relatives and friends that he had left on the Emerald Isle and despite her own bitter feelings towards him, Sheila wanted to make his final weeks as comfortable as possible. As she tossed and turned, flinging the bedding around as she lay thinking, a firm decision was made. Sheila would help Roland to care for his father and confront her own demons in the process.

At daybreak, Sheila Hannigan sat carefully applying her make-up and wig to transform herself into Gipsy Rose. She would be glad when she could finally take off the itchy nylon hairpiece for good but today was all about keeping up pretences and maintaining a level head. She drank two strong cups of black coffee and ate a piece of buttered toast. As she heard the familiar roar of Roland starting up his pick-up truck, Sheila grabbed her handbag and slipped seven sealed envelopes inside. It hadn't taken her long to write the messages but, now that she had, it was like a great weight lifted off her shoulders. She zipped the bag closed and went outside to meet Roland who was smiling at her through the driver's side window.

"Are you alright darling?" he asked as Sheila climbed up beside him, "You look as white as a ghost."

"It's bloody freezing so it is," Sheila cursed, rubbing her hands together, "Turn the fan on."

Roland obliged and shook his head, it didn't matter how much Sheila Hannigan cursed and swore he'd always admire her. There was something wonderful about the way in which she approached life, in a no nonsense matter of fact way. Although he could imagine that Sheila could make a man's life hell if he got on the wrong side of her. Maybe it was the woman's brash manner that had made his father warn him away from

Sheila but more likely it was the age gap. It didn't matter, she was a diamond and the young ringmaster couldn't imagine his life without her. Today he would talk to Patrick and tell him that they needed Gipsy Rose to leave Hannigan's Circus. Roly O' Hare needed a nurse.

Gipsy Rose had a steady stream of customers that afternoon, some wanting their palms read and others preferring to be fore-told their destiny by the turning of Tarot cards. It didn't matter to the psychic which method she used, as she knew the fate of her clients the moment they entered her tent, but she was there to provide entertainment and hope, never failing to disappoint. By lunchtime, Sheila was more than ready for a cup of tea and took her flask and sandwiches outside into the fresh air. The sky was a deep grey and as Sheila stood contemplating whether to go back inside, the first flutter of icy snowflakes landed on her cheek.

"Would you like to eat your lunch in the warm?" a voice called, "You can use my trailer if you like."

Sheila turned slowly and came face to face with her father, "No, I couldn't," she babbled, "I mean it wouldn't seem right, I'm alright here, I can go back in the tent so I can."

"Nonsense," Patrick insisted, "I'm off on an errand anyway, go and sit by the fire for half an hour."

"Well, if you're absolutely sure Mr. Hannigan," she simpered, "Thank you very much."

Sheila couldn't believe her luck. This was exactly the opportunity to go inside Patrick Hannigan's trailer that she'd been looking for and she hadn't even had to ask him!

Waiting until she was sure the circus owner had gone, Sheila turned the lock on his caravan door and began looking around. There on the shelf was a photo of her parents in their court-ing days, her father sporting the same thick moustache that had now turned grey and her mother wearing a traditional Romany costume, similar to the one that her daughter now wore as part of her disguise. Sheila could see a great deal of herself in the pretty woman that stared back at her from the picture and the thought of her mother's demise made her even more determined to carry out her plan.

Patrick Hannigan wasn't the tidiest of men, and Sheila had to move a great deal of clothing and newspapers off the bunk to find what she was looking for, careful to remember the exact way the items were arranged, so that the owner wouldn't detect any disturbance on his return. Lifting up the foam topper of the integral seating, Sheila lifted up the lid of the bunk's storage compartment and peered inside. Immediately she saw what she was looking for. It lay in the same place that it had done ten years before when she had lived here with her parents, although the leather on the huge box was more worn these days from not being polished. Carefully lifting the lid as she also cautiously listened for noise outside, Sheila removed the black cloth and stared down at the contents.

Rose Hannigan's crystal ball lay undisturbed in its velvet tomb, protected by a layer of padded fabric and hidden safely away. As Sheila touched the glass orb with her fingertips, she felt something akin to a static shock as the energy surged through her. This was what she wanted. Patrick had refused to let his daughter take her mother's prized possession but now she would take her inheritance and use it in the way in which her destiny foretold.

Glancing at the clock on the wall, Sheila realised that ten minutes had passed already and she still had to return the caravan to its original state. Carefully lifting the crystal ball from the box, she wrapped it in the surrounding fabric and laid it on the floor next to her. However, glancing down into the bottom of the leather casket, Sheila noticed a piece of thin cardboard placed over the bottom of the box, which she hastily removed and then sucked in her breath at the sight of what lay underneath.

There were thousands and thousands of pounds in ten pound notes, all wrapped in bundles with a sticker in her mother's handwriting attached to the top of each. Sheila flicked through one of the bundles and estimated it to be about three thousand pounds, the others looked to be exactly the same. She turned the piles around so that she could read the writing properly and cursed that she hadn't brought her spectacles.

"Patrick, Eamon, Sean, Dermot, Daniel, Steven, Sheila," she read slowly, hardly believing what she was seeing, "There's one for each of us."

Outside the engine of Patrick Hannigan's Land Rover could be heard coming to a stop.

"Alright Rose?" the circus owner asked as he opened the trailer door, "You must have warmed up nicely as your cheeks are all flushed so they are."

"Yes, thank you," the fortune-teller smiled," quickly checking her handbag to make sure she'd zipped it up.

"Oh, you needn't have tidied up," Patrick told her, glancing at the neatly folded clothes on the bunk, "But thanks anyway, this place could do with a woman's touch."

Sheila stood up to leave, lifting the heavy bag onto her shoulder, "Well, I'd best get back to work."

"Jeez, you women and your handbags," Mr. Hannigan laughed, "You could keep the kitchen sink in there!"

"Indeed," Sheila chuckled, brushing past him, "And a lot more besides."

The rest of the day passed in slow motion for Gipsy Rose. She didn't want to raise suspicion amongst her co-workers, or her new boss for that matter, and continued to see customers until Roland came for her at nine o'clock that evening. Most of the performers, and the circus owner, were still inside the main tent as the show still had another half an hour to run, but Sheila didn't want to hang around.

"I saw Patrick earlier," Roland told her, "He's okay with you finishing. Did he say anything?"

Sheila shook her head, "No, but it's fine, shall we just get going?"

"Don't you want to say farewell to the others?" the man asked, "We can hang on a while."

"No," Sheila replied firmly, tugging at the wig, "Let's just go. And Roland, I think we should make one last move tomorrow. I've an uncle with a farm in Tipperary, your Da will be more than comfortable there."

"That sounds great, will your uncle be alright with that?"

"Yes," Sheila smiled, "My Aunty Di has sorted it all out."

Later that night, as they dismantled Gipsy Rose's purple and gold tent, Sean and Steven Hannigan found that the fortune-teller had left something behind. Six white envelopes with the names of each Hannigan brother written boldly on the front sat on the fortune-teller's table. Inside was the number of a P.O. Box in Tipperary where their sister would be able to receive mail for the next three months, should any of them wish to make contact. Each note explained the reason for Sheila leaving and their father's part in her sadness, a secret that she'd never had the opportunity to tell them before.

It was several days before Patrick Hannigan discovered the missing crystal ball and bundle of cash and when he did open up the leather box, a white envelope was waiting inside.

'Dear Da', it read, 'I have only taken what was rightfully mine and no more, that's what Mam would have wanted. I'm sorry that I came here through dishonest means but I can never forgive you for denying me my rightful future. Maybe now things will be different. Don't try to find me, as you at least owe me the chance to put things right in my life. Your daughter, Sheila."

Chapter Twelve

Roly O' Hare

"Merry Christmas everyone," Seamus O'Leary roared across the long oak table to his guests as he raised a glass of white wine, "Now tuck in and enjoy."

"Merry Christmas," the group chimed, "Thank you Seamus."

Sheila Hannigan took a few minutes to cut up Roly O'Hare's meat and vegetables before sitting down to her own turkey lunch. Roly had become much weaker since they'd arrived at her Uncle's house but, stubborn as he was, the old man insisted that he was alright.

"Stop fussing woman," Roly grumbled as he picked up his fork, "I can manage."

Roland Junior gave Sheila a wink across the table, he knew that his father wouldn't manage without her.

"Pass down those sprouts," roared Seamus, "And don't be shy at filling your plates, there's plenty more so there is."

Sheila smiled, this was just like the family celebrations that she so fondly remembered from her childhood and her uncle hadn't changed a bit in all those years. Still as tall and strong as ever, Seamus O'Leary had the rugged rouged cheeks of a farmer, although she also suspected that his pink tinge could have been aided by habitual whisky drinking too. Seamus was her mother's brother and bore a striking resemblance to Rose, it had been a crushing blow to the man when she passed away. Uncle Seamus had a bonnie wife called Mary and it was thanks to their generosity that the group had been able to stay for the winter. The couple hadn't been blessed with children and doted upon Sheila. It was only after several late nights of sitting up by the fireside that they now knew the truth behind their niece's disappearance after her mother's death and yearned to help her rebuild her life in any way possible.

"Will you stay on with us after Roly's gone," Aunt Mary asked quietly as the women washed the dishes later, "We've missed you so much darling girl."

Sheila sighed and shook her soft brown curls, "I'm so sorry, my home is with the circus now and I miss the friends that I've made. Besides, there's another reason I have to stay."

Mary glanced out of the window to where Roland had gone out to feed the chickens and shrugged her shoulders, "You could both stay here indefinitely, if you wanted to."

Sheila wiped a plate and thought hard about the implications of staying with her relatives. She hadn't been able to spend time with Danger McDougall or Simone during her weeks at 'Hannigan's Circus', it just wouldn't have been a prudent move to reveal her disguise in case her father had questioned them, but by the time they returned to England in the spring, the baby would be born and she would become a godmother. If she were totally honest with herself, Sheila had missed the constant vying for her attention between Ray and Jake too. It was unlikely that she would ever become romantically involved with either of them but it was good to have options.

"No," Sheila finally told her aunt, "Besides, the longer I stay here, the more likely my Da will discover where I am. I did a daft thing taking that money Aunt Mary, but I didn't see any other option."

"You have no reason to feel guilty," the kindly woman told her as she dried her hands, "Besides your Ma left that money for you, Patrick Hannigan had no right to keep it."

"True, and I'm going to carry on the inherited gift of second sight that my mother gave me."

"Well, in that case," Mary sighed, "Let's make the most of the time we have left together."

By New Year's Eve, Roly had taken a turn for the worse and a doctor had to be called. The man had lost his appetite and was much more lethargic than the previous week. The medic confirmed everyone's fears that the circus owner didn't have long to live.

"I'm so sorry Mr. O' Hare," he told Roland out of earshot, "But it really is a matter of days now. Would you consider having your father moved to a hospital?"

"No, that's not an option," the young man insisted, "He's comfortable enough here amongst friends and Sheila can administer his medication."

"Very well," the doctor assented, "Please call me, day or night, if you need me."

"We will, and thank you for coming," Sheila told him as they walked towards the door.

As they reached the end of the hallway, the man turned, shifting his medical bag from one hand to the other, "You do know that Mr O' Hare's condition isn't hereditary don't you?"

Sheila swallowed hard, struggling to maintain composure, "No doctor, I didn't know that, thank you!"

By the fourth day in January, it had been arranged that everyone would take turns to sit with Roly, keeping a bedside vigil to ensure that he was looked after around the clock and also so that Sheila could get some much needed rest after bathing, dressing, feeding and medicating the patient. However, the man's mood was a sombre one and he spent a great deal of time sleeping, but strangely preserving enough energy to have long conversations with Sheila as she attended to him. On this particular day Roly had refused his morning porridge and had asked her to bring a pen and notepad.

"Write down what I tell you," Roly wheezed, "I need to make a stock inventory of all my assets."

"You don't need to be mithering yourself about that," Sheila insisted, "Young Roland can take care of the business. He knows the ropes well enough by now."

"That may be so," coughed the man, lying back against his pillows, "But it's hard work running a circus by yourself and he'll need to keep his wits about him."

Sheila agreed, it was hard work, "I have a proposition for you, to ease the pressure on him."

Roly shifted underneath the bedclothes and squinted at her, "Oh, and what might that be?"

"Let me buy into the business," she said, rushing to get the words out before she changed her mind.

"Where would you get the money to……" he trailed off as a coughing fit began.

Sheila leaned behind her patient, eased him forward and rubbed his back until he breathed easily again.

"I have some inheritance money," she confessed, careful not to meet Roly's eye, "I can use that."

There was no response for a while as the man weighed up his options but finally he started to laugh.

"What's so fecking funny?" Sheila cursed, watching a tear roll down the old man's cheek.

"After all these years," Roly spluttered, "Of me trying to keep you from getting your hands on my boy and now you want to go into business with him."

Sheila narrowed her eyes, the old hatred for Mr. O'Hare welling up inside her again, "I am trying to help him because with you gone that circus will need two minds to keep it ticking over."

Roly shook his head, "I'd rather he sold it on to another buyer than share it with you. Why can't you find a man of your own age to get your claws into Sheila Hannigan?"

The conversation had left a bitter taste in Sheila's mouth. Years of resentment towards Roly had finally begun to take their toll and she didn't know how much longer she could go on caring for him, although perhaps she didn't need to worry too much about the actual duration as the doctor had indicated that they were looking at days now rather than weeks or months.

That evening, Sheila stood outside near the stables smoking a cigarette. She was wrapped up in one of her uncle's heavy jackets but her hands were beginning to turn blue from the cold.

"Whatever are you doing out here?" Seamus called, tramping across the yard towards his niece, "You'll catch your death of cold."

"Oh, Uncle Seamus," she sniffed, "I can't seem to talk any sense into that fool of a man."

"Roly?" her uncle asked, "Well, you'll just have to tell him the truth then."

Back inside, after warming herself by the kitchen fire and preparing a cup of hot milk for the dying man, Sheila tiptoed upstairs to where Roly lay in a guest bedroom. Aunt Mary was downstairs preparing chunks of ham, cheese and crusty bread for their supper and had told her to send young Roland down for a bite to eat when she saw him. Apparently, he'd been with his father for over an hour. As she reached the top landing, Sheila could hear hushed voices coming from the room and paused. She didn't want to disturb the men if they were deep in conversation but being inquisitive by nature, the psychic wondered if Roly was telling his son about her business proposition.

"Why have you left it so long to tell me?" Roland was saying, his voice edgy and full of emotion.

"I didn't think I'd have to," the elder man croaked, "I mean, there really wasn't any need."

"So why now?" the son questioned, spitting out the words as though they were poison.

"Because I'm dying," Roly confessed, his voice shaking, "And that's what people do to ease their conscience on their deathbed. I promise you lad, everything I've done in my life, I've done for you."

"That old cliché" the younger man snorted, "So tell me, where are they now?"

"I honestly don't know," came the response, muffled by a fit of coughing, "I promise you if I did, I'd tell you but as things stand, I wouldn't know where to look."

Sheila Hannigan tiptoed back across the landing and then stamped her foot hard at the top of the stairs, so that the occupants of the room would hear her coming. As she reached the door of the guest room for a second time, it swung open.

"Sorry, Sheila," Roland muttered, running his hands through his hair, "I'm just leaving."

'Don't leave on my account," she smiled, "I've only brought your Da a warm drink, so I have."

"It's alright," he sighed, continuing down the corridor, "We've finished our chat."

"Well," she urged, "Supper's ready in the kitchen, Aunt Mary's set it out by the fire."

The man didn't speak again, but continued on downstairs, only pausing to put on his coat and went out into the cold after slamming the back door.

The following day, Sheila found herself alone in the house with Roly, as her aunt and uncle had gone off to market, taking Roland with them. Seamus had urged the lad to go along with them, pretending that he needed another pair of hands to help with the herd but, in reality, Mary had sensed tension in the air from the previous evening and suggested her husband step in.

Roly had slept for a few hours between breakfast and lunch, although his untouched porridge and cold cup of coffee were testament to the old man's continuing lack of appetite. When he finally opened his eyes again at mid-day, Sheila was sitting beside the bed with a magazine on her lap.

"Where's Roland?" the patient asked, his lips chapped and dry from lack of liquids.

"Gone to market with Seamus and Mary," Sheila told him, wetting the man's mouth with a few drops of water, "They'll not be back until four."

"We had a row," Roly admitted, "And it's my fault."

"Did you now?" the gipsy retorted, raising an eyebrow, "What about this time?"

Roly shrugged, he wasn't inclined to tell his troubles to Sheila, although it might feel good to unload everything onto her broad shoulders, he told himself.

"It's a long story," he mumbled, "You might as well make your-self a cuppa for the duration."

Sheila helped the man to sit up and then pulled the blanket up to Roly's chin to keep him warm. She sensed that this was going to be a long tale and she wanted to make sure that she had a ringside seat,

"When I married Tammy, over thirty-five years ago," Roly be-gan in a croaking voice, "She was everything to me. She was the most beautiful girl I'd ever seen, jet black hair and emerald green eyes, she was bewitching to look at. We hadn't a care in the world, well, except that her parents disapproved."

"But you married her anyway?" Sheila interrupted, shifting in her seat slightly.

"Aye, I did," the man continued, "I was a hard-worker and when Patrick Hannigan and I became business partners, it was a chance to prove to Tammy's parents that I could give her everything in life she wanted. However, as it turned out, the one thing my Tammy wanted more than anything else was a family, and sadly it wasn't to be."

Sheila twitched her lip and watched the man in the bed. He was staring at the ceiling as he talked, and paused for a while as he recalled distant memories.

"Anyway, we tried and we tried, but it just didn't happen. Tammy became depressed and we started to drift apart. If it hadn't been for Patrick's wife, Rose, I think Tammy would have left me."

The old man eyed Sheila who sat patiently waiting for him to continue, "It was actually Rose who came up with the idea of adoption."

"So you adopted Roland?" Sheila asked with a hint of surprise in her voice.

"We certainly did," Roly nodded, "Took him in at just a week old and brought him up as our own."

"How wonderful," Sheila commented, "What about the boy's parents?"

"Oh, we never knew who they were," he continued, pausing for breath, "But that lad hasn't gone without anything, you mark my words."

Sheila looked towards the pillow and could see that the conversation had tired Roly out. She put her hand gently on his arm and whispered to him.

"Get some sleep now, I'll talk to Roland when he comes back."

"I tell you he doesn't know," Sheila insisted as she poured a cup of tea for her Uncle Seamus, "I'm sure of it. I can tell when he's hiding something."

"So what do we do now then?" Mary questioned, pulling out a chair to sit down, "I never thought we'd be in a situation like this. And with that poor man dying as well..."

"That's what makes it worse," Seamus agreed, "We don't have much time to set things straight."

Sheila slumped into a chair and put her head in her hands, "Damn it, what a pickle."

The back door opened, letting in a gust of icy wind and Roland stepped inside. He didn't say anything but pretended to concentrate on pulling off his wellington boots. After a while he looked up at the faces that watched and let out a long sigh.

"Has he told you?" Roland asked.

Sheila nodded, "He has. I'm so sorry."

"Is there any tea in the pot?" the man asked, avoiding her eye, "I'm parched."

"Isn't it time we were milking the cows?" Mary said, nudging her husband.

"We've got plenty of time yet," Seamus replied, but then, receiving a sharp kick from his wife under the table, he added, "Alright, let's go and get it out of the way."

Sheila smiled at her relatives and got up to pour Roland a cup of tea, "Do you want to talk about it?"

He lifted his head and smiled, "No, not really," he admitted, "But I want your help to find my real parents."

"Oh, now hold on," Sheila said calmly, "You need to think things through and talk to your Da again."

"Talk to him!" Roland spluttered, nearly spilling his tea, "Sheila, all my life I've believed that we were kin. That I followed in my Da's footsteps, that we understood each other and that his blood was my blood. Now he tells me that I was adopted. What do you make of that eh? After all the years he's had to tell me, why now? It makes me mad so it does. No, I want to find out about my real family. Will you help me or not?"

Sheila sighed and returned to her seat, "Of course I'll help you, but you need to let me talk to your Da first. Maybe he knows some details that he's forgotten about, I might be able to jog his memory."

Roland put his hand on hers and winked, "You're an angel so you are."

That night, Sheila sat up next to Roly's bed. His breathing was becoming more and more laboured and he was having difficulty swallowing. The doctor had prescribed liquid morphine to drop onto his pillow to ease the pain and the gipsy now dutifully looked at her watch to see if it was time to administer more.

"Are you trying to kill me off?" the old man croaked, suddenly opening his eyes.

"Don't be an idiot," Sheila grumbled, "I'm helping you. Do you want a sip of water Roly?"

The circus owner nodded and lifted his head slightly, allowing Sheila to put a straw in his mouth and once he'd had a brief drink, she seized the opportunity to question him.

"I was talking to young Roland earlier," she told Roly, "He's fair upset by what you told him."

The man lay still but rolled his watery eyes towards her, "I expect he is, but I had to tell him."

"What do you know of his parents?" Sheila pressed, "Do you remember anything at all?"

Roly thought for a minute and then shook his head, "No, nothing, I swear. Rose brought us the baby and she said that she'd signed the adoption papers herself. I didn't ask anything, you know what it's like in our community Sheila, we're under the radar when it comes to the authorities. Moving around every other week, they'd have a hard job to catch us for tax let alone adopting a child."

"It's important to Roland that he finds out about his real parents," Sheila said in a low voice, "Can you think back to the day that Rose brought the baby?"

Roly nodded but the movement caused a coughing fit which took a few minutes to ease.

"I can't remember what was said," he mumbled, "Rose and Tammy were all over the boy, cooing and clucking like a pair of old hens, so Patrick and me went to the pub for a few pints."

"Do you have any of the papers?" Sheila asked hopefully, "Maybe something from where he was born."

"No," Roly insisted, "I don't remember there being any birth certificate. Rose just said he was a week old and Tammy put a mark on the calendar for the lad's birthday. I swear Sheila, there wasn't anything."

Sheila could see that the conversation was tiring Roly out, his lids were starting to close, and she leaned forward to tuck him in properly, "I believe you."

The following morning, after having had a sleepless night sitting up with the patient, Sheila crept downstairs at five o'clock to make herself a coffee. Hoping to have an hour to herself before the rest of the household woke up, she was slightly disappointed to see her Uncle Seamus at the table eating toast.

"Everything alright?" he asked, looking at Sheila over his spectacles.

"Yes, he's asleep," she replied, stifling a yawn, "But I don't think he'll survive another night to be honest."

Seamus made a sympathetic face and got up to give his niece a hug, "You've done all you can Sheila, now sit down and tell me what you and Roly talked about last night."

Sheila repeated the conversation about Roland's parentage almost word for word, emphasising that she thought Roly was telling her everything that he knew.

"You know how it is with my sixth sense," Sheila sighed, "If he was hiding anything I'd be sure to know."

Seamus nodded, "Your mother's daughter through and through, she had incredible powers too."

"Unfortunately, my psychic abilities don't tell me what to do about sorting things out between Roly and Roland," she sniffed, "Maybe I should just do nothing."

"Doing nothing isn't an option," Seamus told her, "Now sit down while I make you some breakfast."

Later that morning Seamus caught up with Roland out on a walk in the fields, he hurried his steps to catch up with the young man and clapped him hard on the back when he did so.

"Alright son?" the farmer roared, "It's a bit breezy out here today, so it is. We're expecting snow later."

Roland pushed his hands deeper into his jacket pockets and smiled, he liked Seamus and Mary, they were good honest folk, "We'd better head back then, unless you needed help out here?"

"No, no," Seamus replied, shaking his head, "I just came out to see if you were alright. Sheila tells me your Da is not doing too well, maybe you should talk to him again, you know, while there's still time."

The handsome youngster looked deep in thought and bit his lip before answering, "You're right Seamus, he's still my Da, after all. I need to set things right between us, who knows how much time we have left?"

"Good lad," Seamus said solemnly, "Let your old man go to his grave in peace."

By the time the men had returned to the farm, Sheila had slept for an hour while Mary sat with Roly and the psychic was now on her way upstairs with a tray containing a cup of whisky and hot water, a bowl of porridge and a fresh, formal writing pad with matching embossed envelope.

"Why don't you let me take that upstairs for you?" Roland suggested, brushing a few flakes of snow off his jacket, "I need to talk to my Da anyway."

"No!" Sheila snapped, but then softening as she heard her own harsh words, "It's a messy job trying to get your Da to eat, so it is. Let me have an hour or so with him and I'll call you when we're done."

"Are you sure?" Roland pressed, "You seem to be dead on your feet looking after him Sheila."

"I'm fine," she smiled softly, "You get yourself warm, Mary's fixing you something to eat."

As she turned towards the staircase, Sheila could hear Roland and Seamus chatting like two old friends. It was the first time she'd heard Roland say more than a few words since the previous day.

Roly O'Hare was asleep. Sheila could tell by his shallow breathing that the old man wasn't pretending and she gently shook his arm to wake him up. He opened just one eye and gave a grunt.

"Wake up Roly," Sheila was telling him, "We need to have a talk."

A slither of spittle rolled down the man's chin but Sheila let it fall until it was absorbed by the blanket and then sat herself down by his side.

"I've brought you some porridge," she told him, but Mr. O' Hare shook his head.

"Whisky and water?" she tried, holding up the cup, "It's your favourite brand."

Roly nodded slightly and a smile crept across his face, "Mmmm," he told her, "Yes."

Sheila leaned her patient forward and let him breath in the whisky before attempting to take a sip, his eyes searching hers as he did so.

"I know," Sheila whispered, "And you need to be patient while I tell you something. Lie back on your pillows now and listen carefully, I'm only going to tell you this once."

An hour later, Sheila left Roly's room with an envelope tucked into her apron pocket. She was exhausted but had to maintain some semblance of normality for the sake of the others. It was Mary whom she came face to face with in the kitchen.

"How did it go?" the aunt asked kindly, as she brushed crumbs from the table, "Is he alright?"

Sheila shook her head, "I've told him everything and he's still in shock."

Mary stopped wiping the table and came to put her arm around her niece, "It was the only way," she murmured, holding Sheila close, "How long has he got?"

"Maybe a few hours, I can feel him slipping away, it won't be long."

Mary O' Leary went to the back door and shouted Roland to come inside, fighting hard to make her voice heard above the howling wind.

"He's gone," Roland said quietly as he entered the room, "But at least we said goodbye."

Sheila didn't move, she was unsure whether to console the young man or not and waited for a signal.

"He was my real Da," Roland continued, his voice still shaky with the shock of this recent revelation, "At least that's what he told me."

Seamus pulled out a chair and guided Roland to sit on it, "He was indeed your real Da."

"I'm baffled," the handsome ringmaster replied, looking from Seamus to Sheila and then to Mary, "First he told me I was adopted and now he's telling me I'm his son. What the hell is going on?"

"I think you'd better go into the front parlour," Mary told Sheila, "Roland, go with her."

The young man followed in silence, confused and wondering what on earth was going on.

Epilogue

Sheila took the envelope out of its hiding place and laid it on the coffee table.

"This is signed by your Da," she whispered, "To confirm that what I'm about to tell you is the truth."

Roland frowned and picked up the sealed note, but he didn't open it, "I'm listening."

Sheila breathed heavily and cleared her throat before embarking on the hardest task of her life.

"When I was seventeen," she explained, "I fell in love with an older man. Being young and stupid, I thought it was the real thing, I would have done anything just to be with him."

"What's this got to do with…."Roland interrupted, thinking he was just about to be regaled with a full account of Sheila's life story.

She held up a hand to gesture that he needed to listen before continuing, "Unfortunately the man whom I was in love with was married, and he had no intention whatsoever of leaving his wife. As you can imagine I was devastated, truly heartbroken.

Roland nodded politely, allowing the woman to continue.

"Well anyway, I didn't realise that my body was changing either," she said, blushing as she recounted the story, "And before I knew it I was five months pregnant."

Sheila swallowed hard, memories flashing into her mind as if it were yesterday.

"My Da went crazy when he found out," she explained, "Threatening me with his leather belt, I swear, if it hadn't been for my Mammy he would have killed me there and then."

Roland stared at the gipsy with wide eyes, not fully comprehending where this was going.

"Anyway," Sheila continued, "My Ma sent me away to stay with her sister, my Aunty Di, as she used to be a midwife. I stayed there until a week after I'd given birth."

"Did you have a girl or a boy?" Roland asked slowly.

"A boy," she replied.

Roland sat in silence as his brain absorbed the details, afraid to contemplate the truth.

"What happened to him?" he faltered.

"My Mammy came and took the baby away," Sheila cried, tears now streaming down her face, "She took him to his father."

She watched the colour drain from Roland's face as he realised the implications of what he was being told and then struggled to carry on with her confession.

"My baby's father was Roly O' Hare," she said, lifting her head, "You are my son."

"But he told me he didn't know...." Roland mumbled, looking at his hands.

"He didn't," Sheila confirmed, "Nobody ever told him. When Mammy took you to Roly and Tammy, she convinced them to move away and make a fresh start. She had enough inheritance from her Da to pay Roly his share of the circus business, so that he could buy his own father's circus."

"What did you do?" Roland asked, "Didn't you want me?"

"I was seventeen!" Sheila sobbed, "I didn't have a choice. By the time I came back from Aunty Di's, your father had moved away. It wasn't until my Mammy died that I plucked up the courage to come and find you."

"And why haven't you told my Da until now?" he questioned.

"Oh love," Sheila said softly, "He didn't care about me. He loved Tammy, I was just a fling and meant nothing."

"And your Da?" Roland asked, "How come he stayed friends with my Da?"

"Because he never knew," Sheila sighed, "Mammy told him it was a lad from the travelling fair that got me pregnant and I went along with it to keep the peace. Can you ever forgive me?"

Roland rubbed a hand over his face and closed his eyes, "And to think I nearly asked you to marry me!"

Sheila touched his free hand and waited with baited breath until the young man relented and got up to hug her, "I am your Mammy," she sobbed, "And I've waited twenty-eight years to do this."

The pair stayed in an embrace until the doctor finally arrived to issue a death certificate for Roly O'Hare.

THE END

About the Author

Having been brought up in a small village in the English countryside, A.J.Griffiths-Jones has plenty of happy memories from which to source information for her novels. However, it's been a long journey. Spanning three decades and two continents, her career & personal life have taken some incredible turns, finally bringing A.J. back to her roots and a promising writing career.

As a young woman, A.J. left the rolling Shropshire hills behind her & headed to London, where she became fascinated in the world of Victorian crime & in particular the unsolved case of 'Jack the Ripper'. Having read every book available to her on the subject, she started her own mini investigation which eventually led to her first non-fiction publication. However, there was a long period of research necessary before A.J. could finally complete her first book and during the intervening years she relocated to China with her husband and took up a post as Language Training Manager for an International bank. As the need for English grew within the company, A.J's responsibilities expanded until she was liaising between two cities and nearly three thousand employees. An initial two year move soon turned into a decade and the couple found themselves in the vast metropolis of Shanghai for a much longer period than they had firstly intended.

Using their Asian home as a base, A.J. and her better half travelled extensively during their time overseas, visiting New

Zealand, Australia, Philippines, Malaysia, Thailand and many provinces within China itself At weekends they would jump into their Jeep and set off to remote villages and mountains, armed with little more than a compass and a map set in Chinese characters, photographing their trip as they explored. Eventually the desire to move back to the U.K. prevailed and the couple returned to their native land in 2012. It was at this point that A.J. made the decision to fulfill her lifetime ambition of becoming an author.

Initially embarking on penmanship in the historical crime genre, A.J. felt it necessary to create a balance between research and writing. The long hours of studying census reports and old newspapers were beginning to take their toll and, having a natural ability to see the funny side of everything, she decided to turn her hand to writing suspense novels with a comical twist. This newfound combination of writing styles has enabled A.J. to get the best of both worlds. For half of her working week she creates humorous characters in idealic locations, whilst the rest of her hours are devoted to research in the Victorian era.

In her free time, A.J.Griffiths-Jones is a keen gardener, growing her own produce and creating unique recipes which she regularly cooks for friends & family. Her plan is to create healthy, filling meals which will eventually be compiled into a cookbook. In her free time A.J. still enjoys travelling, although these days she spends her time visiting Europe and the British Isles, and takes regular holidays in Turkey where she has a relaxing holiday home, which also serves as a haven to complete the final chapters in her books with a glass of wine and a beautiful sunset.

Another of the author's passion's is reading, especially books that take her out of her comfort zone and into a different historical period.

Nowadays, A.J. lives in a Shropshire market town with her husband and beloved Chinese cat, Humphrey. She regularly gives talks at local venues and has also appeared as a guest speaker at New Scotland Yard, where her investigative research was well-received by the Metropolitan Police Historical Society. The author's professional plan is to write a series of suspense novels as well as non-fiction publications relating to notorious historical figures.

Lightning Source UK Ltd.
Milton Keynes UK
UKHW021843141220
375092UK00009B/583/J

9 781034 045106